Looking
for the
Magic

NEW YORK CITY, THE '70S AND
THE RISE OF ARISTA RECORDS

MITCHELL COHEN

TROUSER PRESS BOOKS

"I'll Be Your Mirror" (Lou Reed) lyrics © BMG Rights Management,
Sony/ATV Music Publishing LLC

Design by Kristina Juzaitis / www.FebruaryFirstDesign.com

First Printing June 2022

ISBN 979-8-9856589-0-3

Trouser Press Books

www.trouserpressbooks.com
E-mail: admin@trouserpress.com

TROUSER PRESS BOOKS

To Gayle and Molly

"I'll be the wind, the rain and the sunset
The light on your door to show that you're home"
(Lou Reed)

CONTENTS

Hesh: "There is one constant in the music business...
a hit is a hit. And this, my friend, is not a hit."

Christopher: "Why?"

Hesh: "For reasons we couldn't comprehend or quantify."

—*The Sopranos*, Season 1, Episode 10,
"A Hit Is a Hit," written by
Joe Bosso and Frank Renzulli

AUTHOR'S NOTE

LOOKING FOR THE MAGIC **IS ABOUT ARISTA,** the independent record label—and about Bell Records, its immediate predecessor—so the narrative ends with the conclusion of its indie era in the mid-'80s, when it began being distributed by the RCA branch system. This isn't intended to be a comprehensive account of everything that happened at Arista Records. Some artists who did pretty well aren't mentioned at all, others just in passing (the only place you'll see the names Tycoon and Point Blank is inside these parentheses). It would be foolish to try to discuss everyone who ever recorded or worked for Arista, let alone the vast number of characters and songs that made appearances in Arista's pre-history, on the Bell-Amy-Mala labels and all the labels that company distributed.

Obviously, a good chunk of the label's history happened after the period covered here; Clive Davis's memoir, *The Soundtrack of My Life*, would be the place to pick up the story if you'd like to know more about, say, *The Bodyguard*, Arista Nashville (which deserves a book of its own: Come on, Tim DuBois or Mike Dungan), LaFace Records, or, if you must, Milli Vanilli.

There is some foreshadowing, flashing forward and jumping backward when I think it makes thematic sense. I've tried to make all that as non-confusing and non-jarring as possible. What I've tried to get across is the shape of things: how different genres evolved at the label and what the tone of the times was like, through representative albums and artists. Arista has a reputation as a "pop label," and there's no shame in that: Its pop success was pretty extraordinary. But that's like calling Hachette a "romance" book publishing company because they put out Nicholas Sparks's novels: true but incomplete, since they also publish Malcolm Gladwell and David Sedaris. The film production company StudioCanal, in the first decade of the 2000s, released *Love Actually*, but also *Shaun of the Dead* and *Mulholland Drive*. So think of Barry Manilow as *Love Actually*.

Arista released *Horses*, *Street Hassle* and *Squeezing Out Sparks*; signed Gil Scott-Heron, Anthony Braxton and Iggy Pop; reinvigorated the Kinks and Aretha Franklin; distributed albums by Ian Dury and the Blockheads and the Contortions. Having successful records is always a good thing; that's how the industry keeps score. But often the character of a record label comes into focus on the projects that didn't, in the end, strongly connect outside the company's walls, the ones everyone at the label believed in and fought for in vain. Some of the artists who make appearances in *Looking for the Magic*, like David Forman, Quazar's Glenn Goins, Linda Lewis, and Willie Nile, and some of the albums that came out on the Freedom and Novus labels, are less familiar than they should be. And so much of the pop and soul music that was on Bell Records in the decade between 1965 and 1974 is way too overlooked. This is partially an attempt to fill in those gaps and paint a more expansive picture.

Looking for the Magic. That's a music business job description. You hear a couple of minutes of a demo or catch a few songs of a new artist's live set, and once in a very great while you're struck with what feels like inevitability. And you want everyone everywhere to know about it. This is what Hesh on *The Sopranos* meant when he told Christopher, "A hit is a hit." "Looking for the Magic" is also an object lesson on the capriciousness of the record industry. It was the title of the third and final single released from the Arista debut of the Dwight Twilley Band. The band seemed to have it all: hooky songs, star presence, critical acclaim. But all the label's efforts didn't make one bit of difference. The record flopped. This book is about both sides of the search for magic, the times everything clicked into place, and the times nothing did.

I worked at Arista for a good chunk of the time covered in the book, so I was an observer and/or a participant during some of the events described here. I've kept my personal experiences out of the narrative, but if a sentence reads something like "a number of Arista people," I might be among those people. Not always, though.

Working at 6 West 57th in the late '70s did feel like being part of a New York City cultural renaissance. Not to over-romanticize, or to claim any exclusivity; I know my friends who were at Elektra, Sire, and Island felt the same way, that it was an exciting time to be out in the street, going to CBGB, the Bottom Line, Seventh Avenue South, the Lone Star, JP's, Hurrah, or across the Hudson River to Maxwell's in Hoboken. There was so much going on: no wave, Latin jazz, disco, punk, cabaret. There was a collective feeling that Manhattan was exactly the right place to be, in all its pre-Giuliani seediness and despite its financial travails. (You know the HBO series *Vinyl*? It was nothing like that. People in film and television attempting to capture the NYC music biz get that era wrong all the time.) On the cover of its March 29, 1976 issue, *The New Yorker* ran the famous Saul Steinberg illustration "View of the World from 9th Avenue," where the whole country west of Manhattan is condensed into a small strip of land adjacent to the Pacific Ocean. It was funny because it felt true.

FLASH-FORWARD: SOMETHING SHIMMERING AND WHITE

THE SEA GODDESS, A CRUISE SHIP RUN BY THE CUNARD LINE, had a capacity of 112 passengers on three decks, and for five days in December 1988 every cabin was occupied by employees of Arista Records. It departed from St. Thomas and sailed around the Caribbean. If you see photographs from that trip—a dozen people, male and female, carousing in a hot tub for post-midnight "departmental meetings"; passengers, slathered with sunblock, sprawled in lounge chairs out on the deck and around the pool, in swimming trunks and bikinis—you might wonder what business got done, whether this "convention" was just an excuse to get out of town, soak up some sun, and run up a record-setting tab for alcohol. (At one point, the ship ran out and had to make a stop to restock.) One Arista promotion executive says, "I know there were some wives that were, like, 'You're going on a *Caribbean cruise??*'" *Billboard* headlined its reportage of the event "Arista Hosts Buoyant Meet," and the mood on board was certainly celebratory because, as the song lyric goes, it was a very good year.

Clive Davis's record company, which had just turned fourteen years old, was racking up some formidable statistics. Early in 1988, Whitney Houston broke a record by landing her seventh consecutive single at number-one. (That was cause for another party, as the Arista staff met up at the Cadillac Bar in Chelsea in Manhattan, where circulating servers—called "shooters"—poured tequila shots ("slammers") down the throats of revelers, some of whom did one shot for each of Houston's chart-toppers.) Her second album was on its way to sales of over twenty million worldwide. The year before, Aretha Franklin solidified her stunning comeback with a number-one pop hit—her first since "Respect"—with "I Knew You Were Waiting (for Me)," a duet with George Michael, and had a number-one gospel album with *One Lord, One Faith, One Baptism*. Patti Smith, after a long break from recording, returned in '88 ("People Have the Power" made its debut on her *Dream of Life* album, and became a song of lasting resonance). Carly Simon won an Oscar for "Let the River Run" from the *Working Girl* soundtrack; there were credible rock albums by the Cruzados, Stealin Horses, and the Church; and a lot of Top 10 pop hits. A *lot*.

A half-decade earlier, the company was in no position to fork over $100,000 to sail around the Caribbean. Arista's marketing meetings in 1983 took place in the Catskills, at the Nevele Hotel, a resort that had, to be honest, seen better days when it was a getaway for cost-conscious summerers who couldn't quite afford Grossinger's. There was something bleak and a little shabby about the '83 meetings, a feeling that the label needed a jump-start. There had been a recent internal reorganization, along with a switchover from independent distribution to RCA's branch system. But all that uncertainty was a faint memory when Arista got on board the Sea Goddess. Davis took the podium in an auditorium with a bruising chill-factor (employees knew to attend Davis's meetings with sweatshirts, and some brought blankets to bundle up in), and you could see how invigorated he was, how eager to share all the positive financial news, to extoll the merits of his staff and his artist roster, to introduce upcoming music.

Davis invited a few of his execs for a private lunch in St. Barts (one remembers it as being at Le Sereno) to fine-tune the boat's musical agenda, confirm what tracks to play. The theme of the convention was "Riding the Wave of Success – Arista 1988," and Davis ticked off all the stats, all the platinum that had been accumulated. In one of his epic multimedia product presentations, he also made sure everyone knew that much was expected in the new year. After an exceptionally successful 1987, Davis had told the *Los Angeles Times*, "You always have to keep proving yourself in this business. If there's the slightest slow period, the knives come out."

In 1989, Arista was going to launch a new label in Nashville under the leadership of Tim DuBois, and Alan Jackson's first single was getting ready to roll out. There was a hot-shot Canadian guitar phenom named Jeff Healey and another Canadian, Sarah McLachlan, with her dreamlike first album, *Vox*. Arista had signed Dion, who was on the brink of being inducted into the Rock and Roll Hall of Fame by Lou Reed, and had an album, produced by Dave Edmunds, wrapping up. There was an act from Germany named Milli Vanilli; just as Arista's convention was getting under way, "Girl You Know It's True" was making its way into the hands of radio programmers. Aretha had done a duet with the Four Tops; there were singles by Kenny G and Taylor Dayne; Arista was going to release the soundtrack album from the blaxploitation parody *I'm Gonna Git You Sucka* with tracks by Curtis Mayfield, Jermaine Jackson, and the Gap Band. Normally, an Arista convention would have had live performances, but it was difficult enough getting all the equipment, rented from S.I.R., set up for Davis's presentation, given the amount of space on the boat.

Even by the indulgent standards of the late-'80s music biz, the Arista convention was an exercise in opulence. One afternoon, the company took over a stretch of private beach on the tiny (three square miles, population around 150) island of Jost Van Dyke, where one could swim out into the sea and have the waitstaff carry trays of drinks into the water, so one needn't go all the way back to dry land for more champagne. Then, back on the boat, in the hot tub, in the middle of the night, still more champagne was ordered from room—in this case, tub—service. No one agreed to go on the record about what went on after that, or about an excursion, during a stop in St. Maarten, to try to locate a weed dealer.

Back when Arista was officially opened, in the fall of 1974, at 1776 Broadway in the Manhattan office of what was until then known as Bell Records, the few dozen employees were part of something that looked risky, even given Clive Davis's remarkable run at CBS Records. He'd been running this giant record company, with all the resources and clout that system brings with it, and now he was starting over, testing his ability to find and identify talent and break records without being able to marshal an entire network of CBS branch distributors. He had a lot to prove to a very fickle, judgmental music industry, and it was not going to be simple. There were years when the Nevele would have to do. Now, in 1988, he and nearly everyone who worked for him were on a luxury yacht. On the island of Jost Van Dyke, bubbles of champagne mixed into the cool, shimmering waters, and Arista employees ate lunch and played volleyball on the white sand.

LA BELL EPOQUE

IT WAS A SCENE FUELED BY CHUTZPAH. In midtown mid-century Manhattan, independent record companies, song publishers, songwriters, managers, a Runyonesque cavalcade of hypesters and hustlers all scrambled to make hit records. Every week, the music business trade magazines kept track of who was up and what was coming up, trying to give some semblance of order to what was, essentially, a bunch of guesses. The thing about this world was that chaos was its default mode; office doors were kept open because, well, you never knew who might walk in with some demo or hastily/cheaply recorded master tape or acetate, what a cappella group of boys from the Bronx or Brooklyn might wow you with a song or a sound. Hits came from everywhere, and within days, you could be dropping off a 45 at WINS so Murray the K could hear it, at WMCA for the Good Guys, who might make it a Sure Shot, at WABC, that 50,000-watt behemoth of pop that usually waited until records had gotten some traction elsewhere but might take a shot. Who knows? This record could make the Silver Dollar Survey and earn everyone a few nickels. As music biz kingpin Morris Levy was known to say, those nickels added up.

Bell Records, its sister labels Amy and Mala, and the slew of smaller labels it had distribution deals with, was on a tear in the second half of the 1960s. Bell was in the hit-singles business: Del Shannon's blasts of frantic desperation, "Stranger in Town" and "Keep Searchin' (I'll Follow the Sun)," that foreshadowed *Born to Run* by a decade; Mitch Ryder and the Detroit Wheels, whose records had an uncontained rock'n'roll frenzy; Lee Dorsey's infectious soul, backed by the unerring beat of the Meters. They released "The Letter," "Angel of the Morning," "G.T.O.," "Walking My Cat Named Dog," "I'm Your Puppet," "A Lover's Concerto," and the garage-rock staple "Little Girl" by the Syndicate of Sound.

Bell president Larry Uttal was clever enough to invest in behind-the-scenes talent. Ryder, Norma Tanega, and the Toys came from the house of producer Bob Crewe. Uttal made a deal with Marshall Seahorn and Allen Toussaint to distribute their New Orleans–based R&B label, Sansu. He forged an alliance with the hit-making crew at American Sound Studios in Memphis, who delivered him the Box Tops and Merrilee Rush, and did a deal with Nashville record-maker Bill Justis, producer of Ronny and the Daytonas. If a producer or producing team showed potential, Uttal would try to have that source feed into Bell-Amy-Mala.

This wasn't how business was conducted at most labels. Companies had in-house A&R (Artists and Repertoire) staff to scout, sign, and develop new talent, choose the material if the artist didn't write, select a compatible producer, oversee the recording process start to finish. Uttal did away with all that. He didn't have a head of A&R, and he didn't make records. He made deals with people who made records. As he told *Music Business* magazine in September 1964, what he offered these entities was, "...the greatest exposure possible...[W]e also offer something else to our indie producers, complete artistic freedom. They record what they want, who they want, and how they want to do it. I'll give them advice if they ask for it, but I feel it's their job to make the product and ours to expose it. In a sense we try to work at Amy-Mala like United Artists Pictures. We finance the sessions and give the producer a royalty, but we don't tell them how to make the product."

Jeff Gold, a music archivist, record executive, and Uttal's son-in-law, says, "In all my life, I've never heard of anybody who had that philosophy. Totally unique and completely brilliant, to find these guys who had hit factories of their own to be his A&R company." This was a pretty radical approach, but it paid off; in 1967, Bell Records was named Outstanding Record Label of the Year at the annual Bobby Poe radio convention.

Uttal, born in New York City, had been part of the music business since the 1950s. He tried songwriting ("Can I Tell Them That You're Mine?" by Margie Rayburn on Capitol in '56), sold a master he cut by an artist named Johnny Oliver, "Tom, Dick and Harry," to Carlton Records in 1958, worked as a song-plugger for the Monument Music publishing company, then started his own label, Madison Records, with offices at 1650 Broadway, one of the addresses where the action was (it's where Don Kirshner was building his Aldon publishing empire). Madison began with rockabilly by Billy McBride, a twinkly girl-group record by the Perri's ("Jerrilee"), and the Wild Tones' "Shut-Ups" and "Sick Chick," clicking in 1959 with the Tassels' "To a Soldier Boy" and the timeless instrumental tittyshaker "Harlem Nocturne" by the Viscounts. There was a Top 20 version of "Alley Oop" by Dante and the Evergreens, produced by Herb Alpert and Lou Adler (the Hollywood Argyles had the bigger single), and "Finders Keepers," a Frankie Avalon-ish lament sung by "Herbie Alpert." In a move that predicted his A&R philosophy at Bell, Uttal tapped Alpert and Adler to run the West Coast office of Madison Records in L.A.

Madison released an early single by Ellie Greenwich (under the name Ellie Gee and the Jets), Bronx doo wop by Nino and the Ebb Tides, and "Motorcycle" by Tico and the Triumphs. ("Tico" was one of the pseudonyms Paul Simon was using at the time, as was "Jerry Landis"; he later released singles under both of those names on the pre-Uttal Amy and Mala Records.) "Motorcycle," in 1961, was the last 45 the company released (there were only two LPs, by the Viscounts and Dante and the Evergreens) before Uttal had to shut the label down that fall. There was a small article on page 4 of the October 23 issue of *Billboard*: "Madison Records, Larry Uttal's label, folded last week when the Internal Revenue Department levied the assets of the firm for back taxes. The Internal Revenue

Department [sic] will liquidate the assets of the firm to pay the debts due it. Any additional monies will then be paid to creditors."

Undeterred, Uttal started a new label a month later: Mr. Peacock. He brought along Nino and the Ebb Tides and the Viscounts, and signed Hiawatha Brown ("Hiawatha Doo-Wa"), Lord Didd and the Didn'ts (Lord Didd was frantic DJ Pete "Mad Daddy" Myers), and the Capris. Mr. Peacock was short-lived, however: There was already a Peacock record label in Houston that had been around since 1949, and its owner, Don Robey, wasn't too thrilled that Uttal had adopted the name. Mr. Peacock became Mr. Peeke, but by mid-'63, that incarnation folded. Uttal's next endeavor was to take over Bell Records, whose slogan in the '50s and up until 1960 was "Music for the Millions." It began as a children's label, and then specialized in making knockoff covers of contemporary hit records, sold at budget prices. Mala and Amy, subsidiaries of Bell, were formed in 1959 and 1960, respectively, and neither was catching fire, despite records like "He Won the Purple Heart by Doing the Twist" by Herbie Jay and "Get Up and Do the Wobble" by Paul Simon as Tico (not a Triumph in sight). There were a number of records that have shown resilience, like sides by Bunker Hill and the Ramrods, but Uttal didn't have much to work with.

"Our first move," Uttal recounted in a *Record World* magazine interview, "was to sign a major artist of the day, Del Shannon. This not only provided us with a big hit, 'Handy Man,' but demonstrated to distributors and the industry that we knew what we were doing. It made them take us seriously at once." Uttal also reiterated his strategy of outsourcing: "By limiting our output to records from the indie producers, Bell has a totally sales- and promotion-oriented staff, and can concentrate on the business side." What Uttal built in the second half of the '60s was a consistent hit-churner, with a particular focus on R&B. (Bell got in the game a few beats too late to snap up any unclaimed gems from the British Invasion. As NYC rivals like Laurie and Kapp got Gerry and the Pacemakers and the Searchers, the closest thing to a first-wave U.K. hit on Amy was the Adam Faith rouser "It's Alright.")

Uttal told *Record World* in 1966, "I have been admiring the product that has come out on Atlantic, Tamla-Motown, Chess and Checker, and so forth. In my admiration of their

product, I was aware of my inability at the time to create good R&B records that could not only compete, but that would not be inferior or insincere." The initial move in that area was to pick up Larry Maxwell's Maxx label, which brought along Gladys Knight and the Pips ("Giving Up," "Either Way I Lose"). Lou Johnson came through a brief deal with Big Hill/Big Top Records that provided records produced by Burt Bacharach ("Always Something There to Remind Me," "Kentucky Bluebird"). Uttal got James and Bobby Purify from Papa Don Schroeder; Lee Dorsey (and a whole lot of other A-level New Orleans talent, like Aaron Neville and Betty Harris) from Seahorn and Toussaint; James Carr on Goldwax; the Delfonics on Philly Groove; Al Greene (who would later drop the final "e"), and the Soul Mate's on Hot Line.

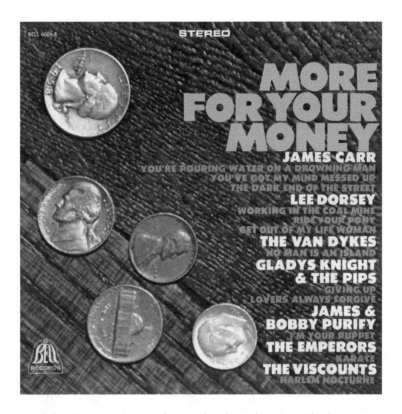

All of which was mighty impressive, and over the decades, even the less commercially viable Bell-Amy-Mala soul records have been reignited by R&B-centric scenes like the Beach Music fervor on the Carolinas coast of the U.S. and, especially, the Northern Soul network of clubs in Great Britain. Singles like the O'Jays' "I Dig Your Act" (before they joined the Gamble and Huff roster), the Van Dykes' "You're Shaking Me Up," and the Masqueraders' "How Big Is Big" (from Tommy Cogbill and the Memphis studio crew) rose from relative obscurity to become reliable "floor-fillers." On online auction websites, 45s like Bernie Williams's "Ever Again" and the Hy-Tones' "I Don't Even Know Your Name," which went unnoticed in the '60s, are now pricey collectibles (someone recently paid more than five grand for the Bernie Williams single). Uttal was so adept at swooping in and signing deals that it got one of his

Bell Records President Larry Uttal presents a gold record to Alex Chilton of the Box Tops onstage at the Arthur Club during a 1968 Bell Records press party in New York.

major rivals, Jerry Wexler at Atlantic, rankled. Wexler wanted the Purifys' "I'm Your Puppet" for Atlantic, but Schroeder had given his verbal okay to Uttal. Wexler was dumbfounded: "Papa Don, are you crazy?" Wexler is quoted as saying. "Don't you realize this is *Atlantic Records*?" Wexler was also ticked off that the Memphis guys behind the Box Tops' "The Letter"—Dan Penn and Chips Moman—didn't bring that single to him, and that they went ahead and made a label deal with Bell for A.G.P. Records (that stood for American Group Productions, named for the studio where the Memphis cats were churning out hits). When you're outplaying Atlantic in the R&B world, you'd better be taken seriously.

Uttal didn't sit still. Not long after taking over Bell, he acquired, at bargain prices, the musical assets of Bobby Robinson's Fire and Fury and Al Silver's Herald and Ember record labels, stocking the Bell vaults with valuable R&B, blues, and vocal harmony records (and reissuing them on the newly formed Sphere Sound label), with a non-altruistic assist from the industry's well-connected rabbi Morris Levy, who allegedly held some markers on the teetering labels. (In later years, when revenue streams from these assets increased during the oldies revival and through usage in films like *American Graffiti*, Levy staked a claim to those snapped-up masters.) As Jeff Gold says, the Uttals used to hang out on weekends with Morris Levy and his wife on Levy's dairy farm. "I asked Larry about Morris Levy," Gold remembers. "He said, 'That's all bullshit, he's not connected with the mob, that's all idle speculation. He'd call me if he needed $50,000 and I'd write him a check and he gave it back to me the next week.' I gave Larry the book *Hit Men* when it came out. He's like, 'Oh my God, I never knew. He was such a nice guy, we were close friends.' It was a fast and loose business at that time."

With staggering regularity, the trade magazines reported that Uttal had made an association with a hot production team/record label. When the F.G.G. (Feldman, Goldstein and Gottehrer) team was heating up, Uttal did a deal with them. (Bell had released their charming Diane Christian girl group singles "Wonderful Guy" and "Little Boy" in '65, and they delivered a remake of "Stand by Me" by Little Eva under the new agreement.) Charlie Greene and Brian Stone were on a high with Sonny and Cher, so Uttal backed their York label. There were Bob Crewe's DynoVoice and NewVoice labels. Uttal picked up L.A.'s Sunburst Records, whose A&R chief was producer Ed Cobb (the Standells), and released singles by, among others, the Standells' Larry Tamblyn, the Zoo ("[Standing on] the Sunset Strip"), and Stark Naked and the Car Thieves ("Look Back in Love [Not in Anger])." He made a deal with Quality Records in Canada to pick up U.S. rights to the Guess Who. Through John Madera Enterprises in Philadelphia, he acquired a single by Daryl Hall and the Cellar Door, "The Princess and the Soldier." Labels came and went: Academy, Aurora (which released the record debut of Al Kooper), Eskee, Round, Elf.

As long as the pop-music business was primarily singles-driven, with airplay on Top 40 radio the goal, the Bell labels would be in okay shape. Singles were economical to cut, and labels could afford to fling them out into the world, cross their fingers, and cut their losses and move on if nothing happened. Mala's version of Bert Berns's "My Girl Sloopy," by Little Caesar and the Consuls, released in Canada on Stan Klees's Red Leaf label, hit the *Billboard* chart the same week that Bang debuted with the McCoys' retitled "Hang on Sloopy" and lost that cover battle. Bell released one-offs by groups like the Changin' Times (a studio creation of Artie Kornfeld and Steve Duboff, courtesy of Kama Sutra Productions), the Chartbusters, and the Dedications (who became the Soul Survivors). You could even give away a singles deal as a prize in a contest, as Bell did with a New York-based group called the Doughboys (originally the Ascots), whose story is typical of Uttal's laissez-faire A&R-once-removed practices.

Group member Richard X. Heyman recalls, "*Disc-o-Teen* was a music TV show that broadcast weeknights out of Newark, New Jersey. It aired on Channel 47, which was a UHF channel. The host was a ghoulish character named Zacherle. The show featured a live studio audience of teenagers frugging to the latest pop hits. A different group from the tri-state area performed each night in a year-long Battle of the Bands contest. The Ascots appeared on *Disc-o-teen* several times as part of this competition ... The Ascots sailed through the first round into the semi-finals, and then came the big day, the showdown with the two other bands who'd made it to the final finals." With a version of the then-

brand-new "Paint It Black," the Ascots won the Battle of the Bands, and the chance to cut a record. They never met with Uttal or visited the Bell offices. Instead, they were signed to Real Good Productions—a company owned by the Brooklyn-bred Jerome brothers, who'd worked with the Left Banke and Reparata and the Delrons—and given a demo of a song by genuine music-biz-crazy Tony Bruno, "Rhoda Mendelbaum." Even fourteen-year-old Heyman knew it was a "lost cause," but they cut the song, had their name changed to the Doughboys, and, "We struck a little deal with WMCA, the New York-based AM station. If we would play their WMCA Good Guys shows every weekend while the record was out, they in turn would give us airplay. Which they supposedly did."

Bell made a deal with Bill Medley of the Righteous Brothers to produce the Blossoms featuring Darlene Love and acquired a bunch of acts that had track records on the pop charts: the Music Machine, Bruce Channel, Shirley and the Shirelles, Reparata and the Delrons (in England and Europe, "Captain of Your Ship" became a hit for the Brooklyn girl group), and Nino Tempo and April Stevens, none of whom (despite fine 45s like the Shirelles' "Look What You've Done to My Heart," written by Ellie Green-wich, and Nino and April's medley of "Sea of Love" and "Dock of the Bay") were able to bring them renewed success in the U.S. Increasingly, the pop music business was an album-based economy, and in that world, Bell struggled to be competitive. In 1968, Uttal took out a trade ad: *"Look: we've come up with something bigger than a Bell single! Bell albums!,"* spotlighting releases by the Box Tops and Merrilee Rush, along with LPs by the English novelty trio Scaffold, singer-songwriter Bobby Russell, James Carr, the Zoo, and the debut by Spooky Tooth, an English rock band—one of the rockiest acts on the label, in fact, since the Syndicate of Sound—that Uttal had picked up from Is-land in the U.K. One track on *Spooky Tooth* was a Vanilla Fudge-y slow-motion take on Janis Ian's "Society's Child," thus managing to combine two tributes to Shadow Morton in one track.

Uttal was spending more and more time in Bell's London office ("He was there all the time," his daughter Jody Uttal recalls), and he was making more deals with labels and producers over there, getting U.S. distribution rights over the next few years for Larry Page's Page One Records, Dick James' DJM, and acts produced by Mickie Most and Tony Macauley. As intent as he was on maintaining Bell's track record in black music—in a *Record World* article, he proclaimed 1968 to be the "Year of R&B"—he knew he need-ed to tap the market for English rock and pop, so he went on a little spree: Nirvana (the '60s U.K. one, with the theme from *The Touchables*), Plastic Penny and Vanity Fare (from Larry Page's Penny Farthing imprint), early U.K. rocker Billy Fury and, through U.K. publisher Dick James's company, British thrush Cilla Black, who made her label debut with "Step Inside Love," a song gifted to her by Paul McCartney.

It was obvious that Bell's methodology needed some tweaking, and it wasn't as though Uttal wasn't giving it a shot. Bell released, in 1968, a completely disarming, intimate album by Margo Guryan, *Take a Picture* (she'd written songs like "Think of Rain" and "Sunday Mornin'," getting her lots of covers and, in the latter case, a single by Spanky and Our Gang), recorded in New York City with such ace session men as keyboard player Paul Griffin and drummer Buddy Saltzman. That same year, Bell made a deal to distribute Bobby Darin's Direction Records; Darin, devastated by the assassination of Robert Kennedy, recorded a so-serious, reflective collection of original songs, *Bobby Darin Born Walden Robert Cassotto*. It might not have been the album Uttal had in mind when he decided to

sign Darin, but he put his stamp on it: "It reveals a side of Bobby Darin's personality that has never been heard by the public before. And it will no doubt surprise some listeners, because the total effect of the album poignantly passes on to them Darin's sense of personal involvement in the world today. Darin's material and performance runs much deeper than the type of music that, up to now, has been his signature. The album expresses the personality of a mature artist in a perfectly realized creative whole." The earnestness of Darin 2.0 (really, more like 5.0 or 6.0: in ten years, he'd gone through a slew of musical revisions) was awkwardly touching ("How do you kill an idea?" he queried on the album's opening track, "Questions"), but it didn't resonate with his fans, and didn't give Bell the hit LP it needed. Bell Records remained a label that spun at 45 rpm.

PARTRIDGES AND FEATHERBEDS

COLUMBIA PICTURES LAUNCHED ITS RECORD DIVISION IN 1958, the same year the Warner Bros. film studio decided to get into the music business. Colpix Records got off to a shaky start (its debut single was by Eugene LaMarr and His Magic Accordion), but it hit its stride as a platform for some of Columbia's TV and film personalities, scoring hits by James Darren, Shelley Fabares, and Paul Petersen. Colpix branched out with records by Nina Simone, Woody Allen, the Marcels, Duane Eddy, Dick Gregory, and the Chad Mitchell Trio; A&R head Stu Phillips concocted a studio girl group, the Colpixies, and put out his own singles like "Love Theme From *The Guns of Navarone*," that heartstring-pulling romantic film of 1961. In the fall of 1966, Colpix was replaced by Colgems, home of Columbia's TV sensations the Monkees (the label also tried to make a singing star of Sally Field, then the studio's Flying Nun, and Sajid Khan, a *16* magazine cover boy featured on the TV show *Maya*). The label released soundtrack albums: Burt Bacharach's jaunty score from *Casino Royale*, Lalo Schifrin's *Murderer's Row* (as seen in Quentin Tarantino's *Once Upon a Time...in Hollywood*), Lionel Bart's *Oliver!*, Quincy Jones's *In Cold Blood*. While the Monkees were hot, so was Colgems, but the Monkees couldn't last forever.

If the movie studio were to keep pace in the record industry, a more reliable source of hit product would be necessary, and Bell, toward the end of the '60s, was still chalking up chart singles: the Box Tops' "Cry Like a Baby," the Delfonics' "La-La (Means I Love You)," Merrilee Rush and the Turnabouts' "Angel of the Morning." (One early 1969 single that was not a hit came from Uttal's distribution deal with Dick James's DJM Records: DJM/Bell put out "Lady Samantha" by Elton John, but Bell passed on John's album.) For $3.5 million in stock, Columbia Pictures bought Bell Records in March 1969. Uttal commented that the arrangement would provide "areas of exploitation for our present rosters of performers and producers" and "makes it possible for us to attract and develop important new talent that might otherwise have gone to other organizations."

One thing on Uttal's to-do list for 1969 was trying to figure out this whole "underground" thing, which he could see was what the kids were into. *Record World* asked him, "What is your definition of 'underground'?" and he responded, "Very much above ground." He pointed out Bell's forays into this under-above territory, mentioning bands like Smokestack Lightning, Spooky Tooth, Nirvana, and the Zoo (and Elmore James, whose blues recordings on the Enjoy label came to Bell as part of the Bobby Robinson masters purchase). Uttal stuck to his procedural guns, saying "We get our artists from our producers," singling out Chris Blackwell (Nirvana), Jimmy Miller (Spooky Tooth), Bones Howe (Smokestack Lightning), and Ed Cobb (the Zoo). On one of his U.K. trips, he inked two producers, Derek Lawrence and Sandy Roberton. "In the label's first two moves to bow their British Bell logo with local talent," Roberton recalls, "I was running Chess Records' publishing companies at the time and very much trying to break into becoming a producer. I'd produced a couple of artists for Decca, and I was hustling everyone. A publisher in Denmark Street had signed Mickey [Jupp], and somehow I got into the frame and they hired me to produce the album. A young guy I knew,

Trevor Churchill, had just gotten hired by Bell Records, and either I or the person at the production company got the tapes to Trevor, and he signed Legend." Although Legend didn't make much of an impact, the group's singer and songwriter Mickey Jupp went on to become one of the first artists signed in the '70s to Stiff Records.

Uttal finally found his signature rock band when he made a label deal with Bronx-born bassist and producer Felix Pappalardi, who'd worked with the Youngbloods and, most impressively from an on-the-radar perspective, Cream, and artist manager Bud Prager. The first album on Windfall Records was *Mountain*, billed as a solo album by Leslie West, the dexterous, imposing lead guitarist of the semi-legendary East Coast band the Vagrants. The album came out in the summer of 1969, by which time Mountain was a legit band and not a West project, and the band was invited to play at Woodstock in August, landing (not intentionally, the schedule was notoriously a shambles) a prime slot at 9:00 pm on Saturday, in between Canned Heat and a lethargic set by the Grateful Dead. Nearly half of Mountain's Woodstock set—songs like "Long Red," "Dreams of Milk and Honey," and "Southbound Train"—came from the *Mountain* album; a year later, the first proper Mountain-the-band album was issued on Windfall/Bell. *Climbing*, featuring "Mississippi Queen," "For Yasgur's Farm" and "Theme for an Imaginary Western," became a Top 20 gold album, the first rock album on Bell to hit those marks.

"I think it's safe to say we've added successful LP merchandising to our pre-eminence in singles," Uttal told *Cash Box* in the fall of 1969, referencing "fast-rising chart LP's" by the Box Tops (*Dimensions*) and Leslie West (*Mountain*) and strong sales action on albums from Solomon Burke (*Proud Mary*, an impressive reframing of the R&B sultan, recorded at Muscle Shoals' Fame Studios, with appreciative liner notes by Creedence's John Fogerty) and Crazy Elephant, who had what Uttal termed a "soul-bubblegum" hit with "Gimme Gimme Good Lovin'." That seemed more aspirational than actual, but points for aiming high. "We have completely regeared the company from its limited aspect of singles and singles producers," he said to *Billboard* around the same time. "We are now aiming for artists who can make it with albums as well as singles." (In the same article, Gordon Bossin, head of Bell's album department, said, "It would be like hunting a needle in a haystack today to find a good A&R man just for Bell.") As 1969 was winding down, so were Amy and Mala Records, Amy departing with a Lee Dorsey-Allen Toussaint record "Give It Up," Mala with "Turn on a Dream" by the Box Tops. That left the Bell label to carry on alone in the new decade.

On Friday night, September 25, 1970, at 8:30 p.m. ET, the ABC network aired the premiere episode of *The Partridge Family*, a musical sitcom loosely based on the real-life family group the Cowsills (minus an autocratic, abusive dad, which would have made it a far darker show). The stars of this peppy clan were David Cassidy as Keith Partridge, the group's heartthrob lead singer, and Shirley Jones, his actual stepmom. Every week, hijinks would ensue, and the Partridges would play and sing (that is, Cassidy and Jones did, while the other kid-Partridges pretended to). As was the case in the early days of the Monkees (before the four Monkees fought for more creative agency), professionals were brought in to write, produce, and play: the first PF LP featured songs by Mann and Weil, Cashman and West, Tony Romeo, and Wes Farrell (the album's producer), using studio cats from L.A.'s Wrecking Crew—vets like Tommy Tedesco, Joe Osborn, Larry Knechtel, Mike Melvoin, and Hal Blaine. It was, as one might expect, impeccably well-crafted pop, and since *The Partridge Family* was a Screen Gems Television production, a division of Columbia Pictures, the recordings were on Bell Records, a division of Columbia Pictures. Everyone made a great deal of money.

Three Top 10 albums in less than a year, five gold albums overall, then a lucrative David Cassidy solo career. *Come on, get happy!* A new Bell era had, you might say, dawned. Oh, Dawn: This was another stroke of good fortune for the label in 1970. There was this song, written by Toni Wine and Irwin Levine, called "Candida," and to sing it, the producers, the Tokens (for their company Bright Tunes Productions) and Dave Appell (a pop presence since the days of Cameo-Parkway in Philadelphia), got Tony Orlando to do the lead vocal. Orlando had had a brief fling with Top 40 fame in the early '60s with songs by Goffin and King and Mann and Weil, but had given all that up to take an industry gig with April-Blackwood Music. There was no actual "Dawn." It was just a record, but it was a hit record, and so was the follow-up, "Knock Three Times." After a while, everyone figured, *We have a real act here*. First, "Dawn featuring Tony Orlando," then "Tony Orlando and Dawn"—another Bell moneymaker.

Having scored big with Dawn, Bell must have thought, why not Dusk? And so the Tokens (Hank Medress, principally) and Appell recruited Peggy Santiglia, formerly with the Angels, to make some sprightly neo-girl-group singles under the name Dusk. They called on Irwin Levine and L. Russell Brown, the writing team behind Dawn's hits, but none of the songs they came up with ("Angel Baby," "I Hear Those Church Bells Ringing," and "Treat Me Like a Good Piece of Candy") clicked. Another 1971 Bell single of note: "Dayeynu (That Would Be Enough for Me)" by the Playmates, about which *Billboard* wrote, "The hit group of the past makes a strong bid for a commercial chart comeback with this clever, infectious adaptation of a Hebrew classic melody." Because Passover-themed singles are reliable chart-toppers.

For all Uttal's efforts to go underground, the company continued to rely on singles in the early '70s. Albums by the Hamilton Face Band, Rumplestiltskin (an all-star U.K. studio assemblage produced by Shel Talmy, with such members as Herbie Flowers and Clem Cattini), Orpheus, and the Groop all stumbled out of the gate.

One of Bell's most mystifying albums was 1971's *For You*, a spoken-word-with-music endeavor by actor Anthony Newley, wherein he reads the erotic, let's call it poetry, of Jennings Cobb. Among the selections: "Will the Windows Continue to Mock Me?," "Couples—I Do Not Envy Them," "Your Mouth-Shaping Demands of One Syllable," and "The Anatripsis of Love." In his liner notes, Newley explains his creative direction behind the cover: "How about me, totally naked, with a beautiful nude chick, expressing my desire for her?" Done! *Billboard* weighed in, "It's in tune with the *Love Story* flavor of the day

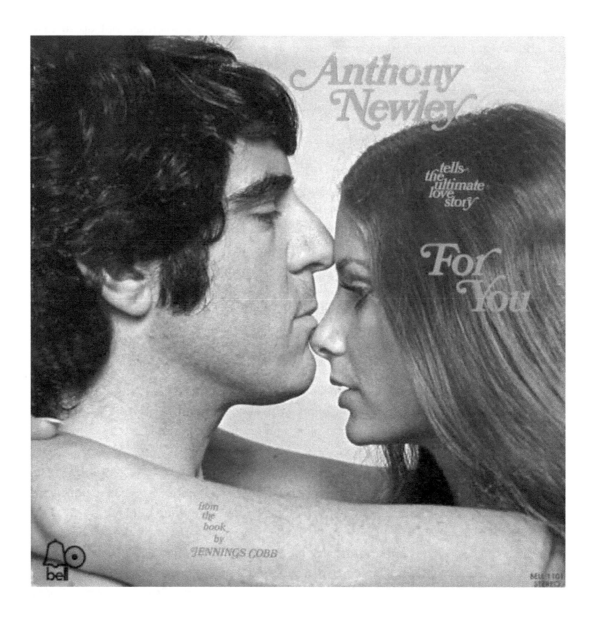

so it should catch on." Background music was provided by Neely Plumb, father of Eve Plumb, who played Jan on *The Brady Bunch*, which preceded *The Partridge Family* on ABC on Friday evenings.

What one might say about Uttal's A&R strategy is that by abdicating the label's decision-making role, except for determining who to get involved with as content-providers, Bell was not in the business of artist development. There wasn't much in the way of follow-through. Consider all the artists who passed through the way station of Bell in one incarnation or another, a stop on the way to bigger things: Elton John, the Guess Who, the O'Jays, Mike McDonald (who released a few Bell singles produced by Rick Jarrard well before joining the Doobie Brothers), Al Green, Daryl Hall, Aaron Neville, Spooky Tooth. And in the early '70s, Bell linked up with other small labels that, had circumstances been only slightly different, could have provided the foundation for a quite impressive Bell profile. In mid-1970, Uttal announced that Bell would be distributing Jimmy Bowen's Amos Records. Although the article in *Billboard* touted Amos's roster as headlining such artists as Frankie Laine and Johnny Tillotson, other records that came through Amos were considerably more promising: Kim Carnes made her label debut with a version of Goffin and King's "To Love"; the group Shilo, produced by Kenny Rogers, featured Don Henley on drums and occasional lead vocals, and he co-wrote such songs as the single "Jennifer (O' My Lady)." Glenn Frey and J.D. Souther's group Longbranch Pennywhistle appeared on Amos/Bell with their joint composition "Bring Back Funky Women," and that's the whole Eagles' declaration of principles right there.

Through another associated label, T.A. Records, Bell had Seals and Crofts. As music biz veteran Dennis Lambert explains, "T.A. Records was formed by Steve Binder, the television director-producer, as an adjunct to his relationship with the parent company... Steve brought me in to run the company day-to-day, mostly focusing on creative issues. I brought Brian Potter with me, as he had just arrived in America from the U.K." Lambert and Potter, who would go on to become a wildly successful writing-producing team, signed the Canadian folk-rock group the Original Caste, who had a hit with the song "One Tin Soldier" from the movie *Billy Jack*. Lambert says that Binder deserves the credit for signing Seals and Crofts, although he got involved to some extent when they were starting to record with producer Bob Alcivar. "The T.A. owners were getting tired of us asking for more funding, especially after Seals and Crofts had a very respectable first album… When the powers that be realized that we were no longer some little side project that Steve could fool around with, they wanted to get rid of the label and its associated costs." The record side of the T.A. deal was shopped to Warner Bros. "T.A. could have been a real player in the indie record world had the owners supported our combined efforts," Lambert says.

You could have hits with Vanity Fare, the Stampeders, Climax, Edison Lighthouse, even with Dawn and the Fifth Dimension (Uttal acquired them through a deal with their producer Bones Howe), and rack up decent market share, but in a post-Woodstock world, the Bell brand was looking slightly antiquated. It didn't help (even though the music was often surprisingly credible) that the acts Uttal was getting from overseas sources like Pye Records, Larry Page, and Dick James looked like the lineup of a British '60s revival tour: the Troggs, Dave Dee, Mike D'Abo, Cilla Black (produced by George Martin), Gordon Waller, Peter Noone (doing a David Bowie tune, "Oh, You Pretty Things"), Twiggy, Paul Jones, Joe Brown, Mungo Jerry, and Status Quo (that would have been a pretty amazing show, actually).

There was the novelty "Johnny Reggae" by British pop entrepreneur Jonathan King, under the *nom du disc* the Piglets, and a remake of the Jamies' seasonal hit "Summertime Summertime" by Hobby Horse, a studio group produced by Tony Visconti (his then-wife Mary Hopkin was one of the session's singers). Uttal took some U.S. shots with early-'70s glam-pop artists from the Bell U.K. roster, like Gary Glitter, Mud, the Sweet, and the Bay City Rollers, who were causing quite the stir in Great Britain but not yet in the U.S. He later made a deal with Mickie Most for a few acts on his RAK label, including the pop-soul group Hot Chocolate, and a feisty expatriate (Detroit-to-London) rocker named Suzi Quatro.

Two New York City-born artists suggested a new course for Bell. Barry Manilow made his first appearance on the label in 1971 as the voice of a "group" billed as "Featherbed featuring Barry Manilow," produced by Tony Orlando; the first Featherbed single was an Adrienne Anderson song, "Amy"; the second was a Manilow composition (with a co-writer credit given to Orlando on the 45, since he tinkered with the lyrics), "Could It Be Magic," with a melody copped from a Chopin prelude. Nothing happened with either single, and Manilow went off to other musical pursuits: commercial jingles and a gig as accompanist and arranger for Bette Midler, a performer who was knocking them dead at the Continental Baths, Steve Ostrow's gay bathhouse in the Ansonia Hotel on Manhattan's Upper West Side, and was signed by Ahmet Ertegun to Atlantic. It was on a jingle date for a Pepsi product that Manilow met Ron Dante, a singer with an extensive résumé in the NYC pop world, from the Detergents to the Archies, with a slew of short-lived solo record contracts along the way (a sampling: Musicor, Columbia, Mercury, Scepter, Kirshner).

Also at that fateful jingle session were singers Melissa Manchester and Valerie Simpson. Dante recalls, "That was the first time, I think, I met Melissa and the first time I met Barry. And we sang our hearts out for the commercial. It sounded great. And after the session Barry came to me and said, 'You're Ron Dante, I know you've had some hits. I'm working with this girl Bette Midler, but I really want to be a solo artist.'" Manilow and Dante arranged to meet a few days later, "and he played me four songs, 'I Am Your Child,' 'Could It Be Magic,' two others. I was producing other people at the time, but I realized what a special voice and what a special person he was, and I said, 'We'll go into the studio, I'll pay for it and let's make some demos to begin with.'" Given Manilow's Featherbed experience, it made sense to approach Bell, where Uttal and VP Irv Biegel were fans. They set up a showcase at the Continental Baths. "I said, 'What is this place, Barry?' He said, 'Oh, never mind. You'll like it.' Barry put together like a 35-40-minute set, Melissa was in the band, I was in the band, and we invited Irv and Larry, and Ahmet Ertegun came, and it was really funny. All the front row was the record people in suits and behind them were guys in towels." Dante recalls that both Bell and Atlantic made

Barry Manilow at home with his beagle Bagel, December 1973

Photo by Linda D. Robbins

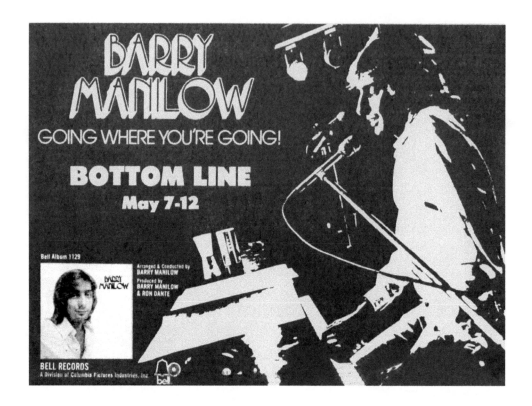

offers to Manilow. "I advised him to go with Bell. You can be the big guy on Bell Records." The deal was announced in the May 26, 1973, issue of *Record World*.

"There was a niche that was not being filled," Dante says. "There was a rise in New York artists at the time. Bette was starting to break through, Manhattan Transfer were starting to break. I thought Barry could be the solo male singer with an eclectic mix of pop songs. We could do jazz, we could do ballads, even a little bit of hep up-tempo R&B. I thought he could cover a lot of things because of where he came out of. He grew up with jazz music from his stepfather. His stepfather played jazz all the time in the apartment, and it was a big imprint on Barry."

Dante and Manilow made the debut album, a collection of engaging middle-of-the-road pop tunes released in the summer of 1973. The only two tracks that Manilow didn't have a hand in writing were the Buzzy Linhart-Mark Klingman song "Friends" that had become a Midler showpiece and "Cloudburst," a cover of the vocalese classic made famous by Lambert, Hendricks, and Ross (Manilow did their "Avenue C" on his second LP). Dante and Manilow also cut a Bell single with actress-singer Sally Kellerman (*M*A*S*H**, *Brewster McCloud*, *Slither*). For her sole release on the label, Kellerman (who passed away in early 2022) did a smoky, slightly psych-pop rendition of the David Crosby song "Triad." "Larry and Irv thought we'd be a good combination for Sally. We met with her and listened to her voice, which is a kind of husky, sexy voice." "Triad," about a suggested threesome, was deemed too risqué when Crosby presented it to the Byrds, then was done by Jefferson Airplane, and Kellerman throatily played up the naughty factor with a knowing chuckle. Under the name Bo Cooper, Dante put out his own Bell 45, "Don't Call It Love," getting a production and arranging assist from Manilow (Bell advertised it as a "career-launching single," ignoring all of Dante's pre-Bo accomplishments).

Barry Manilow wasn't quite Top 40 enough, wasn't nearly rock enough, wasn't really that jazzy overall, so it didn't cause much of a commercial ripple, but Manilow began winning over fans when Midler turned over a portion of her live set to him. Bell took out ads asserting that Manilow was "A Great Performer in the Tradition of Himself!"—a roundabout way of saying, "Look, we're not sure where this fellow fits in, but he's quite entertaining in his own way." Manilow did not lack confidence, on stage or off. There is a famous story of a time that he, Billy Joel, and Bruce Springsteen were sharing a meal in Philadelphia hosted by WMMR radio personality Ed Sciaky, and Manilow announced that he was going to be the biggest star among those at the table. In an interview with writer Arthur Levy in *Zoo World* in late '73, he was considerably more rational. "I wish I was sure I had an audience out there that I could go out and say, 'Hello, how do you do, here's some nice music,' but to go out there and be the warmup act for some comedian doesn't sound too tempting at all. I don't know how well-known I am. I have no idea if they printed 'Barry Manilow Opening at the Troubadour in L.A.' whether anybody would show up or not."

Not long after the release of Manilow's album, Bell put out a single by Melissa Manchester, a version of "Never Never Land" from the musical *Peter Pan* written by Jule Styne, Betty Comden, and Adolph Green. It was a strangely cabaret-esque way to kick off Manchester's big-time record career (there'd been an earlier single on MB Records), especially since she was getting noticed as a writer as well as a performer (she was drawing crowds to Reno Sweeney, the hip nightspot on West 13th Street). She'd been selected to take Paul Simon's songwriting class at NYU in the summer of 1971. As she told an interviewer, "I auditioned for Paul himself. He asked me to play a couple of songs and afterwards he

said, 'Have you been listening to Laura Nyro?' I said, 'Oh, yes, every night and day,' and he said, 'It's time to stop now.'" It wasn't surprising that Manchester saw Nyro as a guiding musical light; for aspiring New York writers of that time, Nyro's distinctive blend of pop and soul, her combination of authenticity and theatricality, was intoxicating, and fellow Bronxite Manchester was one of her satellites.

When Manchester was approached by Bell, she was elated but a little apprehensive. She later said to writer Charles Donovan, for retrospective liner notes, "They were considered a singles label and I was their first albums artist. I had been trying to get a record deal for years...When I was finally signed by Bell Records it was thrilling on many levels." She went into the studio with producers Hank Medress and Dave Appel; typically, Uttal didn't poke his head in to see how things were coming along. "Larry Uttal, the lovely president, had the wisdom to leave me alone. I thought that was what it was gonna be like forever."

To be fair, Manchester wasn't Bell's "first albums artist." By the time *Home to Myself* was released, the label had put out credible albums by Dan Penn (*Nobody's Fool*), Bobby Doyle (*Nine Songs*), and John Hurley (*Delivers One More Hallelujah*). Each was direct and unfussy and can stand with no apology alongside better-known solo albums of the first years of the '70s. Penn in particular, who'd co-written so many major songs for Bell artists—like James and Bobby Purify's "I'm Your Puppet," James Carr's "Dark End of the Street," the Box Tops' "Cry Like a Baby"—made an exemplary LP debut. Uttal, however, was still grappling with how to make the important business-model transition. "Singles are an abstract product," he'd once pronounced, "while albums are a concrete product," a theory that he used to explain how he chose colors for LP covers, but failed to address the underlying issue of musical decisions. In 1973–1974, Bell's product was a typical (for the label) cornucopia of the good (the rambunctious clamor of the Sweet and Quatro), the inexplicable (Rodney Allen Rippy, the Panda People) and whatever Julius Wechter and the Baja Marimba Band performing the theme from *Deep Throat* is. One hit that eluded Bell was 1974's "Love Will Keep Us Together" by the British duo Mac & Katie Kissoon, which the label picked up for U.S. distribution. It didn't catch on (it did do well in the Netherlands), but a year later the Captain and Tennille won the Grammy for Record of the Year for their version of the Neil Sedaka-Howard Greenfield song.

In '73, Uttal addressed NARM (the National Association of Recording Merchandisers) and made some astute observations about the state of the music biz, as well as some predictions. By the year 2001, he said, there would be "completely computerized consumer retail purchases." He tackled pricing ("Do you all realize that the price of singles is the same as when I entered the business in 1955?") and piracy, and foresaw an industry dystopia where independent distributors would go out of business, and as a result "a record industry will emerge in which the smaller company won't be able to exist. It won't be able to compete and will therefore be swallowed up by the con-glomerates."

As for Bell itself, Uttal remained publicly upbeat, declaring the label's first fiscal quarter of 1974 (July–September '73) to be "excellent from every standpoint, and a spring-board for this quarter which has already produced two marvelous months." Among the marvels were "four important new recording artists": Manilow, Manchester, Brownsville Station (a rock band on the Bell-distributed Big Tree), and First Choice (an R&B girl group on Philly Groove). He was looking ahead, slightly concerned about vinyl and paper shortages, but on the whole, facing what he was confident would "prove to be a banner year for Bell Records."

SEA OF POSSIBILITIES

UNLIKE UTTAL, WHO'D BEEN HUSTLING IN THE NEW YORK independent music business since the late '50s and cobbled together Bell-Amy-Mala with acquisitive moxie, Clive Davis, a graduate of Harvard Law School, spent his record biz career zipping up the ranks of CBS Records to run the industry giant's entire record division; Columbia Records, one of CBS's two major labels (the other was Epic), was the home of *My Fair Lady*, Barbra Streisand, Bob Dylan, and Johnny Mathis. It was rich in history, and the halls of Black Rock, its offices on West 52nd Street, were haunted by legends: Louis Armstrong, Billie Holiday, Duke Ellington, Robert Johnson. CBS was, under Columbia's A&R chief Mitch Miller, less than enthused about the whole rock'n'roll game, although it was getting better at it, with Dylan, the Byrds, Simon and Garfunkel, and Paul Revere and the Raiders. On the Epic side, they had the Dave Clark 5 and the Yardbirds alongside Bobby Vinton.

What Clive Davis did was accelerate the push towards rock. He was on a mission to drag the relatively stuffy CBS into the Age of Aquarius, and within a few years, he built up a roster that was, in the fashionable parlance, *heavy*: Big Brother and the Holding

Company featuring Janis Joplin, Sly and the Family Stone, Santana, Mike Bloomfield's Electric Flag. There was jazz fusion and country crossover, there were new artists like Billy Joel and Aerosmith, there was a deal with Kenny Gamble and Leon Huff's Philadelphia International label. And it was all delivered with showmanship and swagger. Davis was happy to assume the mantle of the music industry's most visible spokesperson, touting his achievements and his innovations on matters such as variable album pricing and the phasing out of mono records.

CBS always had clout, but Davis gave it enhanced rock credibility. He was on some kind of roll: Not only was he putting impressive numbers on the board, but Columbia and Epic were recognized for taking chances on artists such as Iggy Pop (*Raw Power*), Mott the Hoople (*All the Young Dudes*), the Zombies (*Odessey and Oracle* on the Date subsidiary), and a young, energetic, and lyrically florid kid from New Jersey, Bruce Springsteen (*Greetings From Asbury Park, N.J.*). That Davis did all this while still micromanaging the roster of middle-of-the-road singers like Andy Williams and Jerry Vale was a remarkable balancing act. Then, in May of 1973, for reasons that, officially, were tied to allegations of misappropriating funds and being connected to some shady music biz characters (like that ever came up when nearly everyone was kissing Morris Levy's ring), CBS let Davis go. What seemed obvious was that, while CBS corporate overlords were all too happy to scoop up the cash generated by Davis's Blood, Sweat and Tears, they felt he was perhaps overzealous in calling attention to himself and running the show however he saw fit. So although he'd made one smart move after another, he was out on the street.

The industry was (1) stunned by his abrupt dismissal, and (2) certain he would land another prestigious gig, because there were any number of record companies that could benefit from savvier A&R and promotion. Guesses were thrown around: partnerships with major movers and shakers like Island's Chris Blackwell or his own label in tandem with an existing powerhouse like Elektra or Atlantic. It's fair to say that picking an association with the record division of Columbia Pictures would have paid off long odds in a Clive Davis Employment pool. Bell was that scrappy singles label at 1776 Broadway. Its roster in the early '70s included Vicki Lawrence and little Ricky Segall from *The Partridge Family* in its jump-the-shark season. It put out records by defensive tackle Rosey Grier and released an album titled *The Jewish American Princess* (track two: "Care and Feeding of Judy Ann Pearlman"). Bell had hit records, all right: Terry Jacks' "Seasons in the Sun," the Sweet's "Little Willy," the slinky-soul of the Delfonics courtesy of Philly Groove. But it didn't have many reliable hit artists, and it didn't move many albums (Tony Orlando and Dawn were doing fine, but they were on their way out the door, contracting with Elektra for future product).

Davis spent the year after his dismissal writing a memoir (*Clive: Inside the Music Business*) and plotting his comeback. Meanwhile, 1974 was not shaping up as the most productive year for Bell Records. Not much was causing a stir, chart-wise. The Partridge Family's streak was ending; most of the glam-rock Uttal picked up from the U.K. (Mud, Suzi Quatro, Alvin Stardust) fell flat in the U.S. (Gary Glitter's thumping "Rock and Roll Part 2" being one notable, fluky exception); Bell in America couldn't get a bite on the Bell U.K. sensations the Bay City Rollers, or Barry Manilow and Melissa Manchester. On the album side, *Free to Be...You and Me*, a collection of enlightened songs and sketches for children, released in 1972, was getting a boost from a 1974 television special, but otherwise, there were things like *Modern Barbershop Quartet* (self-explanatory: the tunes included "Tie a Yellow Ribbon Round the Old Oak Tree," "Delta Dawn," and "Behind Closed Doors"), a live album from David Cassidy that failed to chart, and lingering regrets over the reaction to the soundtrack album from the musical *Lost Horizon*, a catastrophe for Columbia Pictures, Bell Records, and Burt Bacharach and Hal David.

Columbia Pictures was looking to make a change, Clive Davis was available, and Al Hirschfield, the head of the studio, made an offer. On what was very nearly the one-year anniversary of Davis being shown the door at CBS, it was announced that he would become a "consultant" to the music arm of the movie company. As reported in *The New York Times*, negotiations were under way for a "permanent association" between Davis and Columbia, and anyone who read *Billboard* or *Record World* knew exactly what that meant: Uttal was out, Davis was in. But in what? Would Davis go on a talent-raiding binge, wooing artists from his former home or from former competitors? (At CBS, he'd been known to seduce artists—Neil Diamond, Pink Floyd, Ten Years After—away from their labels, and he'd taken Mountain's Windfall Records from Bell.) Tantalizing as that scenario might have been (*Record World* reported that Davis had been seen huddling with Bob Dylan), Davis was quick to point out that it wasn't so simple to extract artists from existing contracts.

Davis's mandate, he always said, wasn't to take over Bell Records, but to build a brand-new independent label, a mini-major, "from scratch." Or at least from scraps. In his new position, he could survey the existing Bell roster and keep whatever intrigued him. The rest would be gone. At CBS, he'd been the captain of a sleek and powerful ocean liner; what Uttal had assembled was a fleet of small speedboats, all racing around in different directions. Uttal's practice of outsourcing A&R to autonomous, self-contained indie operations was an effective strategy in the singles-oriented '60s, but that's not how Davis operated. Every artist, every record, every choice of a producer would have to have his personal stamp of approval, and he started by seeing what he already had on deck.

Okay, what've we got? Orlando and Dawn were planning their exit, but they still owed Bell about two albums' worth of material, so put that aside. Bell had made a distribution deal with Melanie's Neighborhood Records (Melanie had, for a moment, been on Columbia while Davis was there, but her hits, including "Brand New Key," were on Buddah), and there was a chance she could come up with something snappy. There was the Philly Groove label (the Delfonics, First Choice). Lou Rawls, the Fifth Dimension, Al Wilson (on the Rocky Road label), and Peter Nero had, at least, some name recognition and maybe could benefit from Davis's song input. What else? Hanging on to the Bay City Rollers, despite prior U.S. indifference, had no downside: They were signed to the U.K. company, and who knows what might happen? Suzi Quatro looked like a rock star, and Mike Chapman and Nicky Chinn could probably write her a hit. The rest of the Bell roster scattered: Terry Jacks, after the single "Rock'n'Roll (I Gave You

Suzi Quatro performing at the Bottom Line in New York City, April 1974.

Photo by Linda D. Robbins

the Best Years of My Life)," wound up on Larry Uttal's newly formed Private Stock label (as did Mud). Mickie Most's Hot Chocolate jumped over to Big Tree Records and scored with the singles "Emma" (initially a Bell 45) and "You Sexy Thing." Sergio Mendes' brief tenure on Bell ended, and he became an Elektra artist. The Sweet moved to Capitol, David Cassidy to RCA.

What to do about Barry Manilow and Melissa Manchester? Although they'd yet to have their breakout moments, maybe... It certainly wouldn't take much effort to check them out. They were both gigging around town. Manilow had the opening slot for Dionne Warwick at a June 1974 concert in Central Park, and Davis went to the show.

"I remember Barry really knocked it out of the park," Ron Dante says (complete with inadvertent pun). "Vocally, and staging, and backgrounds, and the songs he chose to do. I was on stage with him. We knew we had a great night. After that night, Clive made a really good decision to go big with Barry and move ahead with his career. The Central Park show really motivated him, seeing what Barry could do live."

Davis had no intention of keeping the Bell Records name, which had become synonymous with a tinny kind of pop, a disposability. He decided to call the new enterprise Arista, after the high school honor society he'd belonged to. "Arista" meant "excellence." (It has a secondary meaning, "ear of corn," thus setting the stage for Gino Vannelli, pop music's Fabio.) It is pronounced *A-rista* (the first A as in "Manilow"), although people—like Nick Lowe, who name-checked the label in his industry-jabbing "They Called It Rock"—persisted in accenting the second syllable. (The fact that the new "A" Arista logo was bell-shaped, with a jagged crack, was just a graphic coincidence.) The name does have a certain gravitas, and Davis was not the first person to use it as the name of a record label.

In the 1940s, there was an Arista Records based in Baltimore, which called itself the "top label for Hillbilly Songs and Negro Spirituals." It released 78s by Dewey Price

and His Carolina Hillbillys and the Selah Jubilee Quartet and dabbled in jazz with a record by Don Byas and Slam Stewart ("Slamboree"/"Smoke Gets in Your Eyes"). Later on, in the '50s, there was an Arista Music publishing company based in 1650 Broadway, also the home of such outfits as Aldon Music (Goffin and King, Mann and Weil, Sedaka and Greenfield). Among the songs published by Arista were "Cha Cha Charleston" and "Petite Papillion" by the Three Suns, "Pink Champagne for a Blue Lady" by Al Nevins and His Orchestra, and "Curly" by Sherry Parsons (a trade mag review called it a "pretty three-beater...It's an attractive thrashing job and it merits a listen").

The official unveiling of Clive Davis's Arista wouldn't come until November 1974. In the meantime, he started juggling and expanding his artist roster and hiring staff. Davis moved into 1776 Broadway, and for a while it was a small team. Larry Uttal's assistant phoned Rose Gross-Marino, whose music industry background included a recent stint at RSO Records, to come in to help Davis out during the transition. "I said okay, but only for two weeks. The label was not yet named. I was Arista's first employee. Those two weeks lasted twenty-six years." Of the Bell employees, Davis kept only a few for Arista, including head of sales Gordon Bossin and David Carrico, who was made VP of Promotion. Other key positions were filled by Elliot Goldman (Executive Vice President), Bob Feiden and Rick Chertoff (A&R), and Michael Klenfner (National Promotion Director).

Feiden, who'd come over from RCA Records, was abundantly skilled in the art of the schmooze. ("Bob knew everybody," Gross-Marino says. "He could call anyone in the industry and they would pick up the phone.") He cultivated the refined manner of a socialite in a Depression-era screwball comedy; whether he played squash or not, he always seemed to be coming from or headed for a squash court, and his hours at the office were, or so it appeared, entirely random. Klenfner, a veteran of CBS Records rock promotion, was more of a gregarious bull, hoisting himself onto his motorcycle and zooming around the Manhattan streets like some larger-than-life bike messenger delivering vinyl. And he was one tenacious dude, as fierce about promoting the Bay City Rollers as he was about the Outlaws. According to Gross-Marino, Klenfner was "explosive. You could hear him for miles away. He had a great laugh, a great sense of humor." Together, the Felix and Oscar of Arista were at the center of Davis's brain trust as part of his original team, along with Chertoff, a Philadelphian with strong creative ties to that city, an ear for a commercial song, and talent in the recording studio that would come to full fruition when he left Arista and produced Cyndi Lauper and the Hooters (spun off from his Arista signing Baby Grand) for CBS Records.

Arista's first six months—beginning when it was still Bell in May '74, until the splashy trade launch in November ("Arista: The New Record Company")—were also spent scouting around for talent and making creative moves with the artists Davis kept around. For Manilow, Davis found a song called "Brandy," a minor hit for a British artist named Scott English, and with some modifications and a retitling to "Mandy," it became Davis's first smash on (still) Bell Records.

The whole "Brandy"/"Mandy" situation was a turning point for Davis as a label head. At CBS, artists had success with cover versions—Big Brother and the Holding Company's "Piece of My Heart," Santana's "Black Magic Woman," Blood, Sweat and Tears' "And When I Die"—but those weren't songs that Davis found and submitted to them. He was involved in selecting them as singles, and working on editing and structure, but the material was brought in by the bands.

For Columbia Records' MOR roster, albums consisted of proven songs (Davis would have them record, for example, "Little Green Apples," "Those Were the Days," "We've Only Just Begun"). With Manilow and "Mandy," he pursued a traditional A&R role, as when Mitch Miller would find songs for Tony Bennett and Rosemary Clooney. It was largely what the big-city record biz was built on: song-pluggers trying to get cuts, writers pitching follow-up singles for artists like the Drifters and Gene Pitney (who got to David Pomeranz's "Tryin' to Get the Feeling Again" before Manilow had a hit with it). It became, at times, a tug of war with Manilow and others (Melanie refused to do "Somewhere in the Night"; the Bay City Rollers weren't wild about "Rock and Roll Love Letter"), but it became a defining Arista game plan, Davis finding and stockpiling (he had a running list of songs "on hold" from publishers) potential hits for artists on the label who didn't generate their own stuff (and even sometimes for artists who did).

Spread over two full pages in the inaugural Arista ad was a gallery of the stars in the label's galaxy. There were Bell holdovers like Manilow, Manchester, Melanie, and Peter Nero, whose one Arista LP was *Disco, Dance and Love Themes of the '70s*, with the lead track "Love Theme From *Emmanuelle*," a tune from the gauzy softcore French import

Barry Manilow and Melissa Manchester at the Schaefer Music Festival, September 12, 1975 at
Central Park in New York City.

Photo by Bobby Bank/WireImage

("X Was Never Like This," the tagline promised) that was released by Columbia Pictures in the United States. Arista also put out the movie's soundtrack album, although it missed an opportunity for *scandale* by strategically cropping the topless photo of star Sylvia Kristel that graced the international LP cover.

There were new signings, like Eric Andersen, whose lovely album *Blue River* had come out on Columbia in 1972 under Davis's watch. Andersen, one of the most prominent of the downtown NYC singer-songwriters since recording his debut *Today Is the Highway* for Vanguard Records in 1965, had cut a follow-up to *Blue River* for Columbia, but the tapes got lost (they surfaced years later) and he soon found himself without a label. "Columbia did not renew the deal after they had lost the second album, *Stages*, I had recorded with them in Nashville," Andersen says. "Clive signed me the songs unseen and unheard." Some of the *Stages* songs wound up on Andersen's Arista debut, *Be True to You*, and Davis strongly suggested that Andersen cover the Tom Waits song "Ol' 55." "Jackson Browne and Herb Pedersen dropped by and supplied the Eagles-sound-alike harmonies. At a bookstore in London, I browsed through a bio of Tom Waits and ran across a passage where he said he absolutely hated my version of his song." Waits, Andersen says, once confronted him at the bar at the Troubadour, accusing Andersen of hitting on his girlfriend. "That might be true," Andersen admits.

One newly inked artist who gave Arista immediate credibility came with serious credentials, riveting stage presence, and a way with words. Davis admired writers whose lyrics took poetic turns—he was drawn to Dylan and Paul Simon, and once filmed a video for a CBS convention in which he recited Springsteen's "Blinded by the Light," presenting Bruce at his most linguistically acrobatic—and what could be more perfect for a label with aspirations of grandeur and prestige than a black artist whose songs were streams of sociopolitical commentary over simmering jazz-funk? With his early albums on Flying Dutchman and Strata-East Records, Gil Scott-Heron, born in Virginia but educated at DeWitt Clinton High School in the Bronx and then the elite Fieldston School, was something new. Songs like "The Revolution Will Not Be Televised," "Whitey

on the Moon," "Who'll Pay Reparations on My Soul," and "Home Is Where the Hatred Is," from his 1970 debut *Small Talk at 125th and Lenox* and its jazzier '71 follow-up, *Pieces of a Man*, bristled with anger and wit, and "The Bottle" on '74's *Winter in America* even started to get Scott-Heron radio and club play. Davis went to see a show at the Beacon Theater in Manhattan and, as he told *The New Yorker*, found Scott-Heron "very charismatic, absolutely unique... Seeing him in his prime, the ability to dominate a stage—Gil at his best was an all-timer." Gil Scott-Heron was the first artist Davis signed to Arista. The album, also one of the label's first, credited to Gil Scott-Heron, Brian Jackson, and the Midnight Band, was titled *The First Minute of a New Day*.

The A&R process—discovering, signing, kibitzing, the whole demo-to-master routine—was something Davis was used to. What was less familiar to him was the network of independent record distributors and the power they had to drive a project across the finish line. Making records was one thing; getting them into the pipeline was a different game, and one he didn't have to tangle with at CBS. Running a major record label meant you had your own distributors in place, dealing with retailers, big-box stores, and rack-jobbers, and the agenda was handed down to the field from the command post in New York City. As Rick Dobbis, one of Davis's early hires in the Artist Development department, put it, "We were an independent record company, with independent distributors all over the country for whom we didn't mean anything at the beginning. All of a sudden, there were these people he didn't control, who weren't employees of his, and he couldn't say 'This is the number-one priority for you.' And I'll give him great credit, frankly, for the fact that he made that transition, because Arista would have failed if he didn't make it."

Bell had hits every bit as big as the earliest singles on Arista; there was no difference, really, between "Seasons in the Sun" and "Mandy," "The Night the Lights Went Out in Georgia" by Vicki Lawrence and "Midnight Blue" by Melissa Manchester, or the Sweet's "Little Willy" and the Bay City Rollers' "Saturday Night." The challenge for Arista was to turn chart singles into album sales, and to do that, Davis had to convince distributors to take this start-up label seriously. He gathered all of them in Chicago at the Hyatt Regency O'Hare for a two-day out-of-town premiere of Arista's lineup. They all came: Heilicher Bros. from Minneapolis, Schwartz Bros. from Washington, A&L Dist. from Philadelphia, ABC Record & Tape from Seattle. Davis put on a show, generating excitement for such upcoming releases as the Outlaws, Lou Rawls, the Fifth Dimension, the Headhunters, and Gil Scott-Heron. *Record World* reported that the reception was nothing short of giddy. One of the Heilicher Brothers told the trade mag, "Everyone went away enthused and elated that he will make it all the way." Al Melnick of A&L confirmed, "It's one of the best things to happen to me in 10 years." It took a lot to impress Melnick, but Davis accomplished it by touting Al Wilson and Gryphon.

When he returned to New York, Davis outlined, in a *Record World* interview, how his vision for Arista differed from his predecessor's in the 1776 office ("I don't believe in delegating total creative function to independent producers: You've got to have your own eyes, ears, and A&R men"), and he announced that Arista was already outgrowing its office space and was looking for new Manhattan digs. But that move would have to wait a while.

Arista releases during its first 18 months under new management included a single by New York rock fixture Garland Jeffreys; an album by the Brecker Brothers, Randy and Michael, who were members of the jazz-fusion band Dreams on Columbia (Randy had also been on the first Blood, Sweat and Tears album on that label); the soundtrack albums from Barbra Streisand's *Funny Lady* and *Monty Python and the Holy Grail*; and the original cast album from Kander and Ebb's splashy new Broadway musical, *Chicago*. In the Bell tradition, a few records came and went in an instant: Gold Rush's "Can She Do It Like She Dances," Jefferson Lee's "Maybe I Should Marry Jamie," the Fallen Angels' "The Kid Gets Hot," Cooter Crow & Magic's "Polka Band Hits" (not a polka record, but a breezy-listening easy-rock song *à la* America or Loggins & Messina), the Stanky Brown Group's "Rock 'n' Rollin' Star" (produced by Clive Davis with Jim Mason). Arista also continued the Bell U.K. pickup policy, to a lesser degree, releasing singles by the Glitter Band, Barry Blue, and Showaddywaddy.

Arista signed the captivating U.K. singer Linda Lewis, who came with a chipper song that Cat Stevens had given her, "(Remember the Days Of) The Old Schoolyard." Davis brought her to New York City to record a dance version of the Betty Everett hit "The Shoop Shoop Song (It's in His Kiss)" and a couple of other tracks with the hot production team of Bert DeCoteaux and Tony Silvester. Lewis's record, its title edited to "It's in His Kiss," is a delightful, swirly concoction—one of the most joyful of NYC disco records—and her entire Arista album, *Not a Little Girl Anymore*, is one of the high points of Arista's first year, although Lewis had mixed feelings about the musical direction.

"Arista was more hands-on when it came to choosing material and what have you," she reflected in a *Record Collector* interview. "I saw myself as a singer-songwriter; they didn't. I wish now that I'd enjoyed it more at the time, y'know the riding around in limos, working with the same people who were on Sister Sledge records, recording in New York. Some of the records were really great, I had Luther Vandross as a backing vocalist at one point, so it was all good stuff, but I never really felt it was what I was all about."

Not long after the label launch, Davis became aware of a young woman who somehow managed to weave together the influences of Rimbaud, Cocteau, and Godard into an ecstatic, heightened form of garage-band rock'n'roll. Patti Smith, like Gil Scott-Heron, was a published poet: signed copies of her books *Witt* and *Seventh Heaven* were stacked at the counter of Gotham Book Mart in Manhattan. She was also a playwright (she collaborated on *Cowboy Mouth* with Sam Shepard), and she'd been causing a small commotion with her performances around the city. She was exactly what Arista Records needed; you could not *not* pay attention to her. "It was kind of a strange time," Smith's longtime guitarist-sidekick Lenny Kaye recalls, "coming from a rock perspective, because there were really no rock bands in New York until the glitter scene started happening. It was a very small-scale scene. What there *was* coalescing was a kind of cabaret/folk

Some of the artists featured on the premiere episode of the U.K. pop TV show *Supersonic* in September 1975. One of the first soundtracks released on Arista was from the movie *Stardust*, which starred David Essex and featured new music produced by Dave Edmunds for a fictional group called the Stray Cats.

Left to right: Linda Lewis, David Essex, Gilbert O'Sullivan, Suzi Quatro, Alvin Stardust.

Photo by David Ashdown/Keystone/Getty Images

scene. I remember the Metro on 4th Street that would have folk acts, and it was kind of a cabaret-ish type thing where Patti in the early months would be wearing a feather boa and singing standards with the piano player, and I'd come up and do my two or three scratchy improv poem things."

It started out with little thought about where it might lead. "After the initial poetry reading in '71," Kaye says, "there was no sense that this was a thing that would continue. It was kind of a one-time event. It wasn't until November 1973, which is more than two and a half years later, that she gave a poetry reading at Le Jardin—the rooftop thing at the Hotel Diplomat—and asked me to come."

They did original songs like "Fire of Unknown Origin," "Picture Hanging Blues," and "Ballad of the Bad Boy," and a cover of "Annie Had a Baby" by Hank Ballard and the Midnighters. It was irresistible to the New York rock press, whose ranks included friends and acquaintances of Lenny Kaye, himself a rock writer who worked at the hip record store Village Oldies. By the time CBGB was up and running downtown, Patti Smith already had a following. "Danny Fields had given us some good press in *Soho Weekly News*. Clive is attuned to press, and he came down to see us. We were in the middle of our seven-week run at CBGB, and all of a sudden, the club was filled on Fridays and Saturdays at least, and we were playing four nights a week." There were offers from Audio Fidelity Records and ESP Disk. The ESP deal was tempting, because Smith and Kaye liked the artists on that roster: the Fugs, Pearls Before Swine, Albert Ayler. But a showcase was set up for Davis, who was knocked out, and he signed Smith to Arista. For a while, it looked as though Atlantic's Tom Dowd was going to produce the album, but when that fell through (Mick Ronson, then Ian Hunter's guitarist and co-producer, was also under consideration for a bit), John Cale (formerly of the Velvet Underground) was selected, and Smith and her group went into Electric Lady Studios to record what would become *Horses*, one of the most acclaimed rock debut albums of all time.

Patti Smith and Lenny Kaye at CBGB on April 4, 1975.

Photo by Richard E. Aaron/Redferns

patti smith

Tonight will be a jewel in my crown.
Veins filled w/ existance... beyond race...
gender... baptism. assassinating rhythm.
Hair wires (human light bulbs)

Grace grace greased w/ myrrh + henna.
(the oil the opiate of a woman ascending)
drums. Tongue + waves slapping —

in here lost Tongue Theory.— search for
lost Tongues — Tongue of Tongues — Babel.
Tower crumbling— Tongue extending
Rhythm... motion. Thus the action of language.

The feel of horses long before horses
enter the silence scene,

molten Tar studded (stud—dead) w/ bones
and glass + the teeth of women —

ARISTA

NEW YORK CITY RYTHUM

LIKE MOST RECORD LABELS IN 1975, Arista was creating and/or snapping up disco records. Like the jazz-funk of the Brecker Brothers, the cabaret-pop of Manilow and Manchester, the razzmatazz of Kander and Ebb on Broadway, and the new rock scene that was percolating down on the Bowery at CBGB, disco was part of the aural cityscape. It was still fresh then: Vince Aletti had started writing his influential *Disco File* column in *Record World* in 1974, and the way he described the sounds made it feel like a musical nirvana. There was something seductive about it, even if your tastes ran more to rock, even if you'd never set foot in one of the clubs that were popping up everywhere. Garland Jeffrey's "The Disco Kid" was at least partially tongue-in-cheek, and very entertaining at that, but other Arista records—Jeff Perry's "Love Don't Come No Stronger (Yours and Mine)," Mike & Bill's "Somebody's Gotta Go (Sho Ain't Me)," Harlem River Drive's "Need You," and De Blanc's updated take on Goffin and King's "Oh No, Not My Baby" produced by Chertoff—were one-shots as of-the-moment as the mid-'60s soul sides on Bell-Amy-Mala. Arista also snapped up the infectious dance track "Bump Me Baby" by Dooley Silverspoon.

For a while, before Nik Cohn's piece "Tribal Rites of the New Saturday Night"—the basis of *Saturday Night Fever*—appeared in *New York* magazine in 1976, disco had a nutball dance-craze cash-in spirit, like the NYC music business when enterprising young moguls-on-the-make had offices in the Brill Building and 1650 Broadway, and writers knocked out tunes about doing the Twist and the Hully Gully.

One could imagine, in fact, Manilow and Manchester as part of that lost world. A dozen or so years earlier, they might have taken the subway into Midtown to try to get their original songs cut, maybe become part of a team like Goffin and King or Neil Sedaka and Howie Greenfield. Manilow, in a way, was a Sedaka for the '70s, a Juilliard-schooled, piano-playing Jewish kid from Brooklyn, taking music lessons, throwing bits of classical compositions into his pop songs, becoming a pop star himself despite being blessed with more showbiz moxie than good looks. (It was pure happenstance that Sedaka returned to the charts in 1974 with "Laughter in the Rain," right before Manilow charted with "Mandy.") The difference, obviously, was that Sedaka had his music publisher Don Kirshner behind him, and wrote his own hits, while Clive Davis had less confidence in Manilow's ability to come up with the requisite chart-toppers himself (for one thing, he lacked a lyricist collaborator as deft as Greenfield), so for the most part, Manilow's own songs ended up as LP cuts. As for Manchester, she was in the tradition of Carole King and Ellie Greenwich (with a lot of Laura Nyro thrown in); she even collaborated with golden-era songwriter Carole Bayer Sager, who co-wrote "A Groovy Kind of Love," a hit for the Mindbenders, "Off and Running" for Lesley Gore, and (with Sedaka) "When Love Comes Knocking at Your Door" for the Monkees. Barry and Melissa, in a '60s rom-com, would have met at a song-plugger's office and become a team, professionally and romantically. In the '70s, they met doing commercial jingles and wound up backing up Bette Midler and entertaining an audience of confident men draped only in towels.

To celebrate Arista's first year of operation, and in advance of unleashing *Horses* into the universe, Davis presented a full day of performances—a matinee and an evening concert—at City Center in Manhattan on September 21, 1975. It was billed as a Salute to New

ARISTA RECORDS SALUTES NEW YORK WITH A FESTIVAL OF GREAT MUSIC!

A unique star-studded day/night music festival
of Arista stars celebrating our first year
and the unique vitality of New York music!

A power-packed afternoon concert featuring these exciting contemporary artists:

12:00 Noon

★ GIL SCOTT-HERON & THE MIDNIGHT BAND ★
★ LARRY CORYELL & THE ELEVENTH HOUSE ★
★ THE BRECKER BROTHERS ★
★ JON HENDRICKS ★
★ ANTHONY BRAXTON ★
★ URSZULA DUDZIAK ★

An incredible evening show bristling with great talent:

7:00 PM

★ BARRY MANILOW ★
★ MELISSA MANCHESTER ★
★ LOUDON WAINWRIGHT ★
★ PATTI SMITH ★
★ ERIC CARMEN ★
★ LINDA LEWIS ★

Sunday, September 21, at The New York City Center—West 55th Street
Tickets: $6.50-$5.50 per performance
Available at all Ticketron Outlets and at the City Center Box Office

York (some proceeds funneled to the city, no specific beneficiary), with the afternoon devoted to the artists on the label's jazz roster (including the Breckers, Scott-Heron, sax player Anthony Braxton, and guitarist Larry Coryell), and the after-dinner show devoted to pop and rock. Among the artists at the second show was new signing Loudon Wainwright III, who'd previously made albums for Atlantic and, while Davis was at the helm, Columbia Records. Wainwright was another ideal Arista artist, smart and funny, and there was always the possibility that he would come up with another quasi-novelty song that might be, like "Dead Skunk" on Columbia, a left-field hit.

New York Festival of Music

As I write, three weeks in advance, this has the air of a hype for Arista Records, but it's a good hype—Arista has shown a commendable commitment to New York as a scene, which all proceeds are earmarked to benefit. (But why Eric Carmen, who I love but he's from Cleveland, and not David Foreman, who is still an unknown?) Jazz at 12 p.m.: Gil Scott-Heron, Larry Coryell, Anthony Braxton and others. Pop at 7 p.m.: Melissa Manchester, Loudon Wainwright, Patti Smith, and others. Sunday, 131 West 55 Street. (Christgau) **City Center,   246-8989**

Scheduled for the evening's program but unable to make it (Gil Scott-Heron wound up in the lineup for both ends of the double-header: *Let's play two!*) was Eric Carmen. Davis had flown to Ohio to hear some new songs by the former singer-songwriter of the hormonally amped-up pop group Raspberries, who were critically revered, and signed Carmen to a solo deal. When the *Eric Carmen* album was released in late '75, "All by Myself," a morose (some might say self-pitying) ballad became a huge hit, bringing Rachmaninoff (second movement of his Piano Concerto No. 2) to near the top of the charts. Sergei and Eric had a follow-up hit with the equally sad but slightly jauntier "Never Gonna Fall in Love Again." The album concluded with the Leiber and Stoller/Mann and Weil song "On

Broadway," a hit for the Drifters. It's the definitive song about coming to New York City, where the odds against success are daunting, and the only things you're betting on are your own determination and the way you play your guitar. Arista still had a Broadway address, and like the protagonist of the song, was out to prove the doubters dead wrong. (Years later, Barry Manilow, in concert, linked "On Broadway" to his own hometown tribute "New York City Rhythm," which had been side one, track one on *Tryin' to Get the Feeling Again*, his first album recorded for Arista (his third overall).

Of course, Manilow and Manchester were at the City Center show; they were examples of Arista's alchemy and of a certain branch of NYC pop. Linda Lewis, cited by *New York Times* critic John Rockwell for her "charming stage personality" (he also found Wainwright's songs "wonderfully amusing and perceptive"), was a ray of light, and although her album wasn't quite done yet, Patti Smith was asked to perform for what Rockwell called "her midtown, big-hall debut after a string of wildly successful downtown engagements." As Lenny Kaye recalls, "We were down in Electric Lady recording *Horses*, and we packed up and went up to City Center, go up there, OK, back to the studio: 'What was that about?'" But the Patti Smith Group needed to be there that night. She was, everyone thought, the future of Arista.

Rick Dobbis remembers how Davis presented *Horses* to the Arista staff: "It reminded me of two things when I worked at CBS, the famous singles meeting where he played 'Bridge Over Troubled Water' and when he played [Janis Joplin's] *Pearl*. The presentation was, 'This artist is one of the great artists of our time, and it requires your belief, support, and commitment.' And that's how Patti was presented, as an artist. Not a musical artist, an artist. And the way she was presented to the company was, this was not about hits. That, in itself, was 180 degrees from everything else."

In a *New York Times* Magazine profile of Smith, writers Tony Hiss and David McClelland captured Michael Klenfner in full-tilt promo mode, skillfully walking the hyperbole wire in a call with his team. "[T]his one you've got to handle with kid gloves," they quote Klenfner

"Grace Greased W/Merc And Henna
(The Oil The Opiate Of A Woman Ascending)"

3 Chord Rock Merged With
The Power Of The Word

"beyond race ... gender ... baptism ...
assassinating rythum ... hair wires ...
drums. Tongue and waves slapping ...
molten tar studded—(stud-dead) w/bones
and glass and the teeth of women—
Babel ... Tower crumbling Tongue extending ...
the feel of horses long before horses enter
the scene...."
—Patti Smith

Patti Smith Horses

Produced by John Cale

working the phones, "as tastefully as possible, tastefullier, if possible. ...You have to treat it very gently, we can't just include it with a stack of new releases. If you go in and say, 'I've got the new Bob Dylan,' they'll laugh at you. It's not the new Bob Dylan, it's the new Patti Smith. Patti's not just another artist to me. You always have doubt, but there hasn't been a real good rock chick like this in a long time."

I overslept the day we shot the cover of Horses. I dressed hastily in the clothes I wore, like a uniform, on the stage and in the street. Robert worked swiftly, wordlessly. He had a nervous, confident manner. He had no assistant. There was a triangle of shadow he wanted. The light was changing. The triangle fading. He asked me to remove my jacket because he liked the white of my shirt. I tossed the jacket over my shoulder Sinatra-style, hopefully capturing some of his casual defiance. That was the shot Robert chose.

When I look at it now, I believe we captured some of the anthemic artlessness of our age. Of our generation. A breed apart who sought within a new landscape to excite, to astonish, and to resonate with all the possibilities of our youth.

TALKING BIG APPLE

"I'M BACK," WENT THE RUSS BALLARD SONG that was an Arista single by the U.K. group Hello, "back in the New York Groove!" That record came out at the start of the bicentennial year. What was the New York Groove, anyway? It was the year of Martin Scorsese's urban hellscape *Taxi Driver*—Arista had the Bernard Herrmann soundtrack album, his last film score, as ominous as anything he'd ever done for Hitchcock—and that film felt too close to documentary for comfort to some people. (On the other hand, there was Paul Mazursky's *Next Stop, Greenwich Village*, a valentine to an earlier era in Manhattan.) On Fourth of July weekend, Gil Scott-Heron recorded a live album at Paul's Mall in Boston, and one of the tracks was "New York City." "New York was killing me," the lyric went. Loudon Wainwright III had a song on his 1976 album *T Shirt* called "Talking Big Apple '75," a comic recitation of how dirty and dangerous the city was. Everyone re-membered how, at the end of 1975, President Gerald Ford nixed a federal financial bailout for the struggling metropolis, and the *New York Daily News* headlined a large-font cover, "FORD TO CITY: DROP DEAD."

And yet you could also call that period a cultural revival for the city. *Saturday Night Live* started airing in fall '75; a lot of Arista artists got exposure on the new show, and Arista picked up the first, and to date only, *SNL* cast album. Jann Wenner was making plans to move *Rolling Stone* from San Francisco to Manhattan. The thematic flipside of Scott-Heron's "New York City" was Billy Joel's rhapsodic, Gershwin-esque "New York State of Mind," which appeared, before Joel got around to releasing it, on *Free in America*, a 1976 Arista album by jazz-pop singer Ben Sidran. There was excitement on the East Coast in the second half of the decade, a counterpoint to what had become a numbed-out complacency in, especially, mainstream AOR (album-oriented rock).

What was happening in lower Manhattan was a jolt of musical caffeine, even though, except for Patti Smith, most of the crop of new artists who took over the stage at the end of CBGB's narrow passage past the bar—it was like a sticky road into a cracked version of Oz—didn't impress the squad of Arista talent-spotters. The Ramones were dismissed with barely a glance (how could anyone have missed the irrepressible insolence of that band?); Dobbis recalls bringing Davis down to CB's to see Talking Heads only to be told he didn't know what he was going on about; Blondie ended up signing with Larry Uttal's Private Stock (thanks in part to Blondie producer Richard Gottehrer's '60s Bell connection). In a *Billboard* interview, Bob Feiden had some thoughts on the whole "punk" thing. "The attitude of the bands doesn't yet seem appealing to a broad national front. The punk stance, for example, might be isolating rather than inviting, as in the case of the [New York] Dolls." He also said, "The main thing I find missing though, is songs." His colleague Rick Chertoff wasn't entirely buying it either. "I understand the importance of the punk bands on a cultural level," he told *Billboard*, "but there really has to be a basic musical foundation. I think that the punk bands that will happen in a commercial sense are those bands that bring the attitude and fashions of the new wave together with real music."

Still, Arista had Patti Smith, and that had to count for something, right? Davis also signed Lou Reed who, while the mantle of Godfather of Punk rankled him (most flippant pronouncements did), was surely, with the Velvet Underground, a precursor to the anarchic attitude of these snotty new downtown bands. If the label didn't grasp the exclamatory point that the Ramones and the rest of that Bowery pack were making, you couldn't argue that much of the company's artist roster didn't reflect the stylistic diversity of the city. In 1976, Arista was at the center of New York. Like, the actual center.

Arista found its new offices just steps off of Fifth Avenue, the dividing line between the East and West sides of Manhattan. And if you wanted to mark a halfway point between Gil Scott-Heron's 125th and Lenox and Patti Smith's Bowery and Bleecker, you might wind up on 57th Street. From 57th and Fifth, you were a fifteen-minute cab ride to the Bottom Line, the club on 4th and Mercer that had become the go-to joint for intimate major-label showcases since its opening in 1974. (In 1975 alone, ten Arista artists had gigs there, including the Patti Smith Group with a three-night run beginning the day after Christmas.) A couple of blocks west of Arista's new offices was Carnegie Hall, and just north of that, Lincoln Center. Rose Gross-Marino, Davis's assistant, who made the move with Arista from 1776 Broadway, says that 6 West 57th Street was chosen as the new Arista office because the owner agreed to name it the Arista Building (even though the company would occupy only a few floors at first), but surely that was just a part of it. The whole neighborhood reeked of money and power, and "6 West 57th Street" had such a classy ring to it. It also had history: built in the 1870s by Theodore Roosevelt's father, the family moved there when the future president was fourteen. As a 2005 article in the *New York Times* put it, "One of the best addresses in 19th-century New York was 57th Street from Fifth to Sixth Avenues." It still was a prestigious block when Arista took up residence there in 1976.

Arista initially commandeered 20,000 square feet of space at 6 West 57th (some of its employees were excited to be able to shoot down a few floors to be pampered at the ritzy Pierre Michel Salon which, according to *New York* magazine, was "as crowded at lunch time as Chock Full O'Nuts"). Gil Scott-Heron described the new digs as having "all the clamor of a big city newsroom, bright as daylight with fluorescent tubes running the length of the pathways between cubicles." Also in 6 West was the prestigious Sidney Janis Gallery. "The history of modern-art dealing is unwritten," the *Times* wrote, "and will most likely remain so. But there are places in which it is acted out year by year, and one of them is the Sidney Janis Gallery." In the show Janis mounted in late 1975, "the visitor gets a crash course in Fauvism, Cubism, Futurism, Mondrian and De Stijl, Surrealism and much else besides."

At 16 West 57th Street was the crazily trendy, fashion-forward emporium Charivari; the high-end Henri Bendel was at 10 West. Bergdorf Goodman was on the corner, Chanel and Dior across Fifth Avenue, and the Rizzoli bookstore on the opposite side of 57th Street. Right next to Arista's entrance was the Festival Theater, which had opened in 1963 with the New York City premiere of Fellini's *8½* and continued to program films by directors like Bergman (*The Magic Flute*) and Truffaut (*Day for Night*). (Later in the decade, it became known for Saturday midnight showings of *The Rocky Horror Picture Show*.) Arista staffers discovered, a block away on 56th Street, the restaurant Romeo Salta, about which critic Mimi Sheraton said, "New York has never had an Italian restaurant as good as Romeo Salta was in its heyday."

Davis amped up the release schedule, and the results were hit-and-miss. A couple of singles by Gino Cunico didn't catch fire (although both songs, "When I Wanted You" and "Can't Smile Without You," did not go to waste: Manilow cut them later on). There was a groovy pop album by a band called the Movies, produced by Vini Poncia. Barry Mann, who'd written hit after hit in the '60s with his partner Cynthia Weil at 1650 Broadway, had an amusing single, "The Princess and the Punk," that, sadly, did not become another "Who Put the Bomp" for him. A&R guy Rick Chertoff took General Johnson—the writer-singer behind so many superb records by the Showmen and the Chairmen of the Board—into the studio and co-produced, with the General, an unjustly overlooked modern-R&B album. Chertoff's colleague Bob Feiden was tipped to a New York singer-songwriter, David Forman, whose music evoked memories of the sensuous East Coast post-doo wop produced by Leiber and Stoller, but whose lyrics were vivid and biting.

Purely coincidentally, Forman had released a single on Bell Records, "Tantalize," in 1974, but then was without a label, recording demos that started making their way around the local A&R circuit. "Here's what I think happened," Forman says. "Stephen Holden at RCA tried to get me signed there, and I was so disappointed that he was unable to do that, and Holden said, 'I'm going to suggest that you see Paul Nelson at Mercury.'" There were three or four songs on that demo, including "Dream of a Child," "Smokey China Tea," and "The Marriage of Napoleon," but Nelson also couldn't get his higher-ups to sign off on Forman. As Forman recalls, "Clive had founded Arista, and Feiden had a position there. I think I gave him the tape on a Friday, and it was just like three days later he said he'd played the songs for Clive Davis and he was particularly excited about 'Dream of a Child.'" Arista made what Forman calls "an introductory offer, you know, like the rookie minimum," and Forman became an Arista artist.

A few producers were considered before Joel Dorn was selected. "He had just got done with 'The First Time Ever I Saw Your Face,' and I thought, 'Now that's something I think I can relate to.' It's offbeat and it's beautiful and you never really heard anything like it. It was unapologetically slow-tempo." With Dorn, Forman cut arresting versions of his original songs, and a ballad arrangement of the Goffin and King song "One Fine Day" that had been a jubilant, optimistic hit for the Chiffons. The opening track of the album was the song that caught Davis's ear, the reverie "Dream of a Child," in which Forman summons up boyhood fantasies about Philip Marlowe, Mrs. Mickey Mantle, and Brenda Lee. It's gorgeous, with a tasteful string arrangement and a little Johnny Mathis ("It's Not for Me to Say") piano coda. Maybe it was too abstract and sophisticated to be a hit single, but Arista did try. Full-page trade ads were taken out, and the critics gave it full-throated blessing (comparisons to Randy Newman were thrown around), yet the album made next to zero commercial impact. In a way, though it is a perfect representation of the Arista aesthetic, if such a thing exists. It's lush and literate, with roots in New York pop and soul and a distinctive artist sensibility.

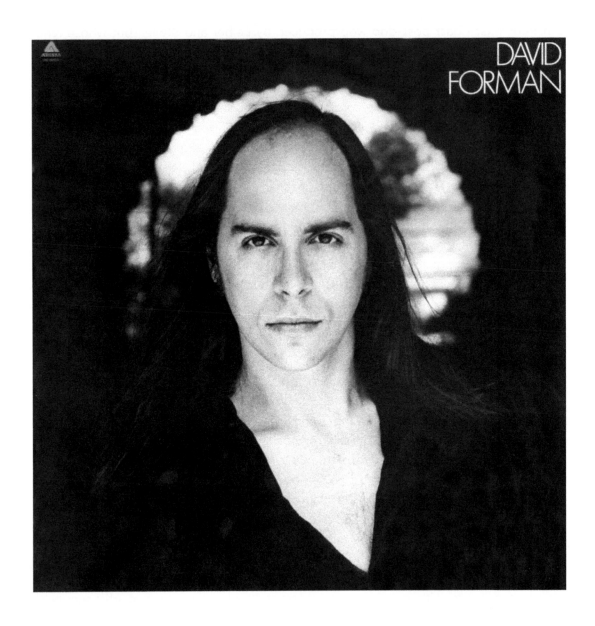

Forman's Arista debut was one of the projects presented to the company at a convention held at the Camelback Inn in Scottsdale, Arizona, in September 1976, along with music from *Rock and Roll Heart*, Lou Reed's first album for the label after parting from RCA Records, the second—at the time untitled—album by the Patti Smith Group, the General Johnson album, and the live double LP that Gil Scott-Heron had recorded in July (*It's Your World*). Davis also showcased, at nighttime live events, newly signed rock bands that had been added to the Arista roster: the British group Mr. Big, the Funky Kings, and the Alpha Band. For the latter two bands, in particular, expectations were high. The Funky Kings featured songwriters Jules Shear, Jack Tempchin, and Richard Stekol. Shear recalls, "Jack, Richard, Doug Haywood, and myself were all playing a hoot night together. I mean, separately, but the same night. I knew all of them except Richard, who I appreciated from his last band (Honk). We were talking after we played and decided to get together to see if we could do something. Doug left, but I decided to hang with Richard and Jack, and what an excellent hang it was. When Clive came to town, he wanted us to play for him, then he signed us and suggested Paul Rothchild to produce."

With multiple songwriters, and Tempchin's recent track record as a writer on a couple of big Eagles songs ("Already Gone" and "Peaceful Easy Feeling"), the Funky Kings were positioned to be Arista's entry into the soft-rock sweepstakes, and Tempchin had written a song, "Slow Dancing," that future Arista A&R executive Michael Barackman, writing in *Crawdaddy*, called "classic prom-pop." But all the windup, including a live K-West 106 radio broadcast from Cherokee Studios in West Hollywood where the band was introduced/endorsed—"A fabulous group that I am totally committed to"—by Henry Winkler (no one was hotter at that moment than the Fonz, with *Happy Days* in its third season), didn't lift the Funky Kings, and it wasn't until Johnny Rivers covered "Slow Dancing" that the song got the attention Arista had banked on.

Davis was also over the moon about the Alpha Band, whose members—T Bone Burnett, David Mansfield, and Steven Soles—had all been part of Bob Dylan's Rolling Thunder

Revue in '75–'76. What could be hipper than that? Maybe they could fill the slot that was about to be vacated by The Band, who were about to scatter after one final blowout on Thanksgiving 1976. Maybe their cerebral lyrics and impeccable musicianship could make them Arista's answer to Steely Dan, who were in the midst of a platinum-album run. They had all the elements that Davis was drawn to—he dubbed what they were doing "surrealist rock," which didn't catch on, but isn't bad—but there was something remote about them, and Burnett's lyrics could get a bit moralizing.

Many critics, including the *Village Voice*'s Robert Christgau ("Finally a decent record comes out of Rolling Thunder," he wrote, calling Burnett an "inspired crazy"), appreciated what the Alpha Band were up to, but except for the *succès d'estime* of *Horses* and pretty fair sales results from the Outlaws, Arista had a way to go before it could claim to have gotten a foothold in rock. For the time being, hit singles by Jennifer Warnes, Eric Carmen, and, most valuably, Barry Manilow (his interpretation of Randy Edelman's "Weekend in New England" would end '76 as his fourth consecutive number-one Easy Listening single) gave Davis achievements to trumpet, as he did when he went on a summer '76 retailers tour that made stops in L.A., New York, Chicago, and Minneapolis, which he said gave him "a unique opportunity to find out what might better serve the industry" and an opportunity to play upcoming product for the retailers.

Arista was still finding its way in 1976. The label signed Martha Reeves, the powerful Motown vocalist, and matched her in the studio with producers General Johnson, DeCoteaux, and Silvester (one of the songs she cut with them was Gwen Guthrie and Patrick Grant's "This Time I'll Be Sweeter," which they'd also done on Linda Lewis's album; Davis did not give up on that song, as we will see later), and Tony Camillo. Rick Chertoff produced a cover of Hall and Oates' "Rich Girl" with Elliot Lurie, who had been the lead voice of Looking Glass. And although Davis didn't follow Uttal's playbook of making deals with many independent content-suppliers, he did sign a distribution deal with Dennis Lambert and Brian Potter's Haven Records, which yielded singles by the

THE ARISTA RECORDS FALL SAMPLER

SIDE ONE
AIN'T IT STRANGE
Artist: Patti Smith

IT'S YOUR WORLD
Artist: Gil Scott-Heron

SLOW DANCING
Artist: Funky Kings

A FOOL IN LOVE
Artist: Melissa Manchester

ROCK AND ROLL HEART
Artist: Lou Reed

WOULDN'T YOU KNOW
Artist: The Alpha Band

SIDE TWO
LADIES PAY
Artist: Lou Reed

INTERVIEWS
Artist: The Alpha Band

LOVE HURTS
Artist: Jennifer Warnes

SWEET MERCY
Artist: Harvey Mason

DREAM OF A CHILD
Artist: David Forman

ASK THE ANGELS
Artist: Patti Smith

FOR RADIO AND IN-STORE PLAY ONLY. NOT FOR SALE.

Righteous Brothers, Evie Sands, Rob Grill & the Grass Roots, and a group called Bandana, which morphed into Player. The Haven–Arista association flamed out quickly and unceremoniously.

Arista felt like Manhattan in those years, with a kind of frenetic, ambitious energy, the way it drew, magnetically, all manner of outsiders from beyond the borough's borders. There is a lot that Barry Manilow and Lou Reed have in common, all musical evidence to the contrary. They were both Jewish, born in Brooklyn; Reed in 1942, Manilow a year later. They'd have heard, as teenagers, music that stirred them, maybe different songs on the same radio stations. Whatever their divergent paths, each spent his early career in versions of the Manhattan underground: Reed in the downtown clubs, Manilow in the baths, playing to clientele that felt like private societies with secrets that the outside world might not comprehend or accept. There were things that linked them—these misfits in the big city—and Melissa Manchester, born in the Bronx, and Gil Scott-Heron, who went to live with his mother in the Bronx when he was twelve years old. Patti Smith, a Jersey girl, moved across the river to New York in 1967, around the same time Michael Brecker came to the city from Pennsylvania. Melanie Safka was born in Queens, Garland Jeffreys in Brooklyn.

Clive Davis, who grew up in Crown Heights, Brooklyn, had as much to prove, and as much determination to prove it, as any of those artists that he signed to his new label. He had risen to the most vertiginous heights of the record industry from those beginnings, was publicly stripped of everything, and now was reinventing himself. Everything was on the line. Maybe that need for revalidation was what he recognized in the artists whose careers were due for a rebooting (Reed, the Kinks, the Grateful Dead, and later Dionne Warwick and Aretha Franklin); he was giving them, and himself, the gift of a second chance. He always looked, when scouting a new artist, for intensity, a performer who had the instinct to seize the moment, as Janis Joplin had at the Monterey Pop Festival, as Patti Smith did almost every night at CBGB. From those impulses, as much from his ability to sense the hit potential of a song from a rough demo, he would make Arista matter.

WE BEGAN!

...with Barry Manilow going straight to number one on the charts, Melissa Manchester moving strongly to the forefront, Gil Scott-Heron hailed as a major artist of the seventies, and our new prestigious Jazz Series critically acclaimed everywhere!

BARRY MANILOW—now one of the hottest artists of '75. His album "BARRY MANILOW II," which was jet propelled by his gold record "Mandy," is sizzling again with "It's A Miracle"! Standing ovations at every show certify Manilow as a major artist here to stay!

MELISSA MANCHESTER has arrived—with style and authority. "MELISSA," her stunning album, is a solid success and her current single "Midnight Blue" is breaking fast as an important chart entry. At 24, Melissa Manchester is assuredly a star

GIL SCOTT-HERON has been acclaimed as an extraordinary artist. His "FIRST MINUTE OF A NEW DAY" album caused music critics — from "Rolling Stone" to "Newsweek" — to welcome him as one of the most important original artists to come along in years. Gil Scott-Heron is not only a musician and a poet; he is a social movement who will shake the heart, the ears and the mind.

ALBERT AYLER, GATO BARBIERI, ANTHONY BRAXTON, MARION BROWN, ROSWELL RUDD, CECIL TAYLOR, CHARLES TOLLIVER, RANDY WESTON—another vital side of American artistry. Arista Jazz albums have sparked the rediscovery of these remarkable contemporary talents.

AND ALL THAT JAZZ

FROM THE OUTSET, DAVIS WANTED JAZZ to be part of the Arista portfolio. It made sense: His experience at Columbia showed him that there was an audience out there. During his tenure, Columbia was instrumental in bridging the rock-jazz divide: Miles Davis made *In a Silent Way* and *Bitches Brew* and started to play the rock ballrooms on bills with artists like Neil Young and Crazy Horse and Laura Nyro. There was an openness, an exchange of musical ideas. What Herbie Hancock, Weather Report, Dreams, and the Mahavishnu Orchestra—all on Columbia in the early '70s—were proving was that jazz could incorporate elements of rock and funk without being clichéd or condescending. A constituency raised on Jimi Hendrix, Sly Stone, and Carlos Santana was prepared to take another step forward, and rock bands with horn sections, like Chicago, Blood, Sweat and Tears, and Chase (also CBS Records artists), started people murmuring about something called "jazz-rock." It was terrain Davis knew, and it fit his idea of Arista being a multi-genre record label.

There were other plusses to consider. Jazz repertoire, from the standpoint of recording and promotion/marketing, was a conservative investment compared to pop, rock, and R&B. Budgets across the board were lower, and you didn't have to sell as many albums to be in the black. Davis could be relatively hands-off as far as the music went, entrusting his jazzcentric hires to supervise and deliver the albums. Realistically, what could Davis do? Tell Oliver Lake to bring back the hook? Ask Airto Moreira to rewrite a bridge? There was no chance Cecil Taylor was suddenly going to be put into rotation on WBLS or WKTU, or even on most jazz stations, so creative interference was pretty much pointless. It was a language other people were fluent in, and it freed Davis to focus on projects with more radio upside. Also, the approval of jazz critics would reverberate, and Davis knew the value of positive press in burnishing the image of his new enterprise. Making an immediate move into jazz—assuming it was the right jazz—drew a sharp distinction from Bell Records, which had never ventured into that territory. It wasn't in Larry Uttal's wheelhouse, and he never made a distribution pact with any label that could add jazz to the Bell roster.

What Arista needed was a jazz guru, and Davis found Steve Backer. At Impulse Records, a division of ABC, Backer had launched an acclaimed reissue series, signed Gato Barbieri and Keith Jarrett and, according to his 2014 obituary in *The New York Times*, "organized a package tour of some of the label's artists, with avant-gardists like the saxophonists Pharoah Sanders and Archie Shepp playing at rock clubs and colleges." These were precisely the kind of credentials Davis was looking for, and Backer became one of his earliest Arista hires. The *Billboard* article that announced the new venture was headlined "Rock, Jazz Seen for Arista Label," and said that Backer "was given a free hand in choosing a number of jazz artists." Backer brought Michael Cuscuna on board. "I got pulled in by Steve," Cuscuna remembers. "We became friends when he was at Impulse and I was at Atlantic and we both wanted to leave and do something together, but it didn't present itself until we were at the 1974 Montreux Jazz Festival together." Cuscuna told Backer at that event that Alan Bates, who owned Freedom Records, was looking for distribution, and that an arrangement like that would give Arista instant catalog.

"Steve wanted to sign Anthony Braxton. When I went to Paris after Montreux, I talked to Anthony and told him to come home, that there were opportunities for him, that this was the place to go." It certainly made a statement, signing Braxton, a sax player and composer whose music was wildly challenging (some might say daunting). Making him Arista's premier marquee jazz artist signaled that, just as Clive Davis had championed Miles Davis at his most experimental, he was prepared to take a leap of faith in Braxton (or at least in the executives who recommended signing him). Cuscuna says, "In our early meetings with just Steve, me and Clive, he made it abundantly clear that he wanted to turn Bell Records, which was becoming Arista, into a major, and that meant he should cover the entire range. So I started preparing releases for Freedom, and also recording new stuff, because that gave me the opportunity to record a lot of my friends like Oliver Lake, Julius Hemphill, and Andrew Hill."

The label now known as Arista Freedom was not an afterthought. It was featured in Arista's trade and consumer advertising: "Arista Records Proudly Presents the Artform of Contemporary Jazz," one full-page Freedom ad exclaimed, with seven LPs displayed and copy praising the "bristling, fluid style" of Charles Tolliver and the "piano tour de force" of Cecil Taylor. Backer and Cuscuna compiled a promotional album billed as "a collection of pieces expressing the more accessible side of the artistry represented in this remarkable group of albums." "Accessible" is relative. In his liner notes, Backer put forth his policy statement: "I'm rather proud of the major commitment Arista Records is making in contemporary jazz in its many forms. We intend to move in many directions in an attempt to bring much of the diverse spectrum of modern jazz to you." The nine tracks on the sampler LP included Roswell Rudd's version of Hancock's "Maiden Voyage" (with vocals by Sheila Jordan, whose daughter

Anthony Braxton's Composition 23 C

ROSWELL RUDD   RANDY WESTON   CHARLES TOLLIVER
GATO BARBIERI   CECIL TAYLOR   ORNETTE COLEMAN
MARION BROWN   ALBERT AYLER   ANTHONY BRAXTON

A collection of pieces expressing the more accessible side of the artistry represented in this
remarkable group of albums.

Tracey would later be a member of Arista's publicity department), a piano solo by Cecil Taylor, a duet ("81st Street") by Gato Barbieri and Dollar Brand, and an Anthony Braxton composition from his first Arista album, *New York, Fall 1974.*

Jazz critic Whitney Balliett, writing in *The New Yorker*, called Arista "a relatively new company that helps mind the avant-garde." "Arista" and "avant-garde" linked in, yes, *The New Yorker*. That kind of recognition is priceless and balances out a whole lot of perceived musical sins. It was a pretty hip place to be: the label signed the rock-fusion band Larry Coryell and the Eleventh House—Coryell had been one of New York's top-tier guitar players since he was a part of Gary Burton's group, then forming the pioneering jazz-rock group the Free Spirits—along with the Headhunters (Hancock's backing group, without Hancock), whiz-kid pianist Herman Szobel, and jazz-fusion artists like Airto, Michael Urbaniak, Larry Young, and Urszula Dudziak. Ben Sidran not only made his own snappy, Mose Allison-influenced albums for Arista, he also produced an album by Jon Hendricks, *Tell Me the Truth*, that framed the vocalese legend as a mod-music pioneer (an influence on artists as different as Barry Manilow and Joni Mitchell) and brought along the Pointer Sisters and Boz Scaggs to help out. And Gil Scott-Heron got enough crossover attention from jazz radio for his albums to show up on the *Billboard* jazz chart. As label gatekeepers went, Backer and Cuscuna were especially attuned to maintaining the integrity of the artists. Cuscuna says, "As far as we were concerned, why would we sign Anthony if we wanted him to be someone else? If I wanted someone to do standards, I would have signed Zoot Sims, you know? The last project we did with Anthony was a three-record set, a piece for two orchestras, 160 musicians that we did in Ohio, and all the way I was flying there I had a smile on my face that Arista was paying for it."

While Arista Freedom took care of the forward-facing side of jazz, Arista also acquired a treasure trove of master recordings by purchasing Savoy Records in 1975. Started in Newark, New Jersey, in 1942 by Herman Lubinsky, Savoy had an astonishing jazz catalog:

THE HISTORIC SAVOY SESSIONS
THE ORIGINAL MASTERPIECES
BY THE LEGENDARY MASTERS
SAVOY SAMPLER

**FOR RADIO AIRPLAY ONLY
NOT FOR SALE**

SJS 01

essential sides by Charlie Parker, Lester Young, Dizzy Gillespie, Stan Getz, Dexter Gordon, Billy Eckstine and His Orchestra, and, as a bonus, stacks and stacks of early R&B and vocal group records by Johnny Otis, the Ravens, Jimmy Scott, and Big Jay McNeely. It was a dream cache of American music, and Backer entrusted its legacy to Bob Porter, who had most recently worked at Prestige Records.

Porter said, in a phone interview for this book (he passed away in April 2021), "Let me explain something about Savoy. Up until about 1950, everything had been recorded on acetate disc; that was the technology at the time. And the acetate discs were in pristine condition, they had been stored in a bank vault for more than twenty years. The tapes, on the other hand, were all over the place, 'cause Savoy acquired a lot of labels in the '50s. They would find somebody's going bankrupt and they would put in a cheap bid and end up with the masters. Some tapes I never found what I was looking for. At any rate, getting started, we did eight double albums as our first release." Among those albums were definitive compilations of Charlie Parker's and Lester Young's Savoy recordings and sets by John Coltrane and Wilbur Harden, Milt Jackson, Yusef Lateef, Cannonball Adderley, and Erroll Garner, along with a multi-artist compilation, *The Changing Face of Harlem*.

Porter's two-disc thematic compilations, among the most entertaining and illuminating of the Savoy reissues, were born out of necessity. "The problem was," Porter said, "Lubinsky was such a prick. Guys would do one four-tune session for him and dislike the experience so much they wouldn't do another one. You had a bunch of stuff like that, so I had to group them in what seemed to be at least a reasonably coherent point of view." Out of that situation came collections like *Giants of Traditional Jazz*, *The Bebop Boys*, *Honkers & Screamers*, *The Roots of Rock'n Roll*, and *Black California*, which brought together sides by Slim Gaillard, Art Farmer, Art Pepper, Hampton Hawes, and others. *Black California* was named by notorious rock critic Lester Bangs as one of his top ten albums of 1976. That was an added-value part of having the Savoy catalog: the Arista publicity department knew, when a new batch of Savoys arrived, writers could be invited up to 6 West

THE ROOTS OF ROCK'N ROLL

THE RAVENS, THE ROBBINS, LITTLE ESTHER, JOHNNY OTIS, NAPPY BROWN, BIG MAYBELLE, HAL "CORNBREAD" SINGER, PAUL "HUCKLEBUCK" WILLIAMS AND OTHERS
THE SAVOY SESSIONS

Everything is rock 'n' roll in 1977. It is either soft-rock or jazz-rock or acid-rock or any other of the seemingly 57 varieties. Yet it wasn't always that way. At the time some of the recordings in this collection were first issued, it was race music. A little later it became rhythm & blues. By the time Alan Freed popularized the term rock 'n' roll, the music had a following. But make no mistake, those of you who may think that rock began with Elvis or (God help us!) The Beatles, the music Alan Freed was talking about already had its own identity. Whether it was a screaming saxophone, a singer shouting the blues, or the mellow laid-back harmony of a vocal group, the music Freed was talking about was Black Music — more specifically, the popular Black Music of the day.

—Bob Porter

SJL 2221

to score the haul, and while there, they could be hyped on other Arista releases. Arista publicist Melani Rogers says she never was able to bring the Savoy albums home, because they were so in-demand by writers. It became a kind of musical lagniappe. Porter says, "We had great press. One guy who helped me in the Arista press department, a guy named Andy McKaie, went out of his way to help with the Savoy stuff, knowing full well that his raise or bonus or promotion wouldn't matter whether the reissue sold. He did it because he loved the music."

Porter had only one meeting with Clive Davis about Savoy, "He was insistent. He said, 'We want to do this right.' He'd come from Columbia, where they had some success with Bessie Smith and stuff like that, so he understood how it worked. I think he was realistic in what the sales potential was. I think we probably did 30,000 on the Charlie Parker double LP, maybe more." The albums were strikingly packaged—Bob Heimall, an art director Davis wooed from Elektra, came up with a bold, modern design for the first Savoys that made them stand out in the jazz racks—and meticulously, passionately annotated. Arista also made certain (in a lot of cases, for the first time) that the financial terms were on the up-and-up. "One of the things Clive did which I really commend him for, he said to tear up the old contracts and issue new ones, which is what he did. So all those Savoy artists started out with a five percent of ninety percent deal. On the one hand, it was great for the artists. Number two, it saved the company a lot of headaches. The other thing that's interesting is that a lot of the Savoy sessions were one-shots. No royalties involved. Some of the guys were making royalties for the first time."

Bird and Pres on one side of the Arista jazz holdings, Braxton and Barbieri on the other, and many attempts to capture the center. Arista Freedom even took a couple of chances with artists that were more mainstream, like the John Payne Band, led by a sax player Cuscuna knew from Bonnie Raitt sessions (he also played flute and soprano sax on Van Morrison's *Astral Weeks*), and a group called New York Mary, co-produced by Cuscuna and Don Elliot, whose résumé included stints with Dizzy Gillespie and Quincy Jones (he also concocted the Nutty Squirrels, a kind of be-bop Alvin and the Chipmunks). Those

acts, which felt more "Arista" than "Freedom," didn't have much impact, commercially or critically. About the John Payne Band, their manager Mike Lembo says, "The jazz snobs didn't like it; it was in the middle. The Headhunters and the Breckers had names. And that was the problem. We did not have a name, but live, this band did very well in the Northeast, in colleges and clubs. It was good money for a jazz artist at their level."

There *were* instances where Davis exercised his A&R prerogative. He convinced Randy and Michael to make an album under the name the Brecker Brothers—it had a marketing hook—even though Randy was mapping out a solo project, and he sent them back into the studio to come up with a track that could be worked as a single. The result was "Sneakin' Up Behind You," and, as he predicted, it was an R&B hit, and the Breckers were nominated for Grammys for Best New Artist (they lost to Natalie Cole) and Best R&B Instrumental Performance (Silver Convention's "Fly Robin Fly" took home that one). The Brecker Brothers were also part of an Arista jazz hub that Backer and Cuscuna were assembling, one that included Bronx-born (from the Dion and the Belmonts part of town) vibraphonist Mike Mainieri, pianist Warren Bernhardt, and guitarists Steve Khan (son of lyricist Sammy Cahn) and Larry Coryell. In 1977, when the Breckers opened their club Seventh Avenue South in the Village, off Leroy Street, that became the unofficial headquarters for this crop of players.

Like the pop and rock coming from Arista in the '70s, the label's jazz side had a decidedly New York tenor—tracks on some of the albums were named "East River" and "Straphangin'" (the Breckers), "Nyctaphobia" (Coryell with Eleventh House), "New York Electric Street Music" (Larry Young's Fuel), "Thurman Munson" (Coryell with John Scofield and Joe Beck) and "Manhattan Update" (Bernhardt)—but much of the Seventh Avenue South gang also had formative roots upstate. Mainieri and Bernhardt were part of the combo that backed up Tim Hardin in the '60s (they can be heard trying to keep up with an out-of-it Hardin on the compelling document *Tim Hardin 3—Live in Concert*). When Hardin moved up to Woodstock, about a hundred miles north of New York City, they decided to make the trek as well. A lively jazz community was taking shape up there, a (very) loose affiliation of NYC expats, and out of various permutations came a Mainieri-driven project called White Elephant, who made one album in 1972 for Michael Lang's Just Sunshine Records. *White Elephant* is a sprawling four-LP session of hippie-jazz-rock featuring Mainieri, Bernhardt, the Breckers, guitarists David Spinozza and Hugh McCracken, drummers Steve Gadd and Donald McDonald (who was in Hardin's backing group), bassist Tony Levin, and about a dozen other players and singers.

"We were all living in Woodstock," Mainieri says. "There was a club up there as important as Seventh Avenue South called the Joyous Lake. Nobody talks about this club. If you had a gig in Boston and you played jazz, blues, rock, your next step would be Joyous Lake in Woodstock, right in town. We had this group for about three or four years, and we started playing at Seventh Avenue South. That's where I met Steve Backer. He loved the direction. We played straight-ahead, we played free, we played something funky. It was what it was. He signed me, and he said, 'What record do you want to do?' I said, 'I have no idea.'" The album he wound up making for Arista was called *Love Play*. "I guess you could call it commercial jazz," Mainieri admits. The LP cover is a photo of Mainieri in a pre-Tony Manero white suit, sitting in contemplation as if he were on *The Bachelor*, deciding who was worthy of the First Impression Rose he's holding in his hands. For *Love Play*, Mainieri called on some of his Woodstock crew (Spinozza, Gadd, McCracken, Bernhardt) and even sang on one track, "Latin Lover." When that song began to get some attention, it also piqued Davis's interest, and he encouraged Mainieri to do more singing on the next album. That advice did not go over too well. "Meanwhile, I'm playing live, and all of a sudden, I have this R&B audience that I never had, and I'm not even singing it. I was too embarrassed."

Around this time, Arista Freedom was being phased out, replaced by a new label for modern jazz called Arista Novus. Backer signed Bernhardt to that imprint, as well as Muhal Richard Abrams, Ran Blake (who made a haunting album, *Film Noir*, for the label), and a blazingly innovative, critically heralded trio, Air, fronted by sax player

Henry Threadgill. Most of the Arista jazz roster, including Pharoah Sanders and Norman Connors, now part of Arista through a distribution pact with Buddah Records, went to Switzerland in July 1978 to perform at the Montreux Jazz Festival.

The weekend of July 21 at the festival was practically wall-to-wall Arista, starting with an aggregation called the Arista All-Stars. "I was musical director," Mainieri recalls. "I tried to help Steve [Backer] in every way I could." He ran the band through rehearsals of songs by himself, Coryell, Bernhardt, Khan, and Alphonse Mouzon, with the rhythm section of Steve Jordan and Tony Levin, and out of that set came two volumes of *Blue Montreux* on Arista Novus. It was an obvious idea to try to make this ensemble a semi-permanent thing, to put together a jazz supergroup like Weather Report or Return to Forever, and Backer pitched it. "I think it was the right idea at the wrong time," Mainieri says. "It would have been amazing. I was into it; I said, 'Yeah, let's do it.' He was a visionary man." But there were all these other projects swirling around, and lucrative studio gigs that would have had to be bumped, so getting the diverse cast of characters to commit to a touring and recording schedule was too much of a hassle. Too bad, Mainieri shrugs. They could have made so much money in Japan.

It was a wild three days at Montreux. In addition to pulling together the All-Stars, Mainieri was given the task of whipping together the players who were going to back Ben Sidran. "Ben got sick the day before," Cuscuna says, "flu or something like that, and he could hardly talk, let alone sing. He was barely getting through the set, so we came back to New York and redid all his vocals. Fortunately, there was enough isolation."

One segment of the Montreux experience never made it to vinyl. Cuscuna explains, "During the day before Larry's performance, we were hanging out and Stan Getz was there. Larry went over and talked to Stan about doing some duets, and Stan said yeah, which is amazing. The art director and photographer came over, and Larry's playing his solo set, and then he brings Stan out. And the fucking photographer crawls right up to their feet, where the fucking motor shutter on the camera destroyed the whole thing. It was louder than the guitar or the saxophone. I was livid."

Despite this mishap depriving posterity of live Coryell-Getz duets, the sets at Montreux were mostly captured without incident. "Montreux was a very inexpensive way to get albums, because they sort of threw in the studio, which was part of the facility. It was dirt cheap; the musicians were already there." On night two, Arista recorded Air (*Montreux Suisse*), solo Muhal Richard Abrams (*Spiral Live at Montreux*), Pharoah Sanders & Norman Connors (*Beyond a Dream*), and a Mainieri-Bernhardt duet set (*Free Smiles*). From the final night, the doctored Ben Sidran set came out as *Live at Montreux*, and sections of the Coryell performance that didn't involve Stan Getz and an over-eager photographer came out on the *European Impressions* album.

There is certainly some incongruity here, a dichotomy that is a bit baffling given Arista's reputation, but during the years when Steve Backer, Michael Cuscuna, and Bob Porter were steering the label's jazz course, no other independent label won more accolades in that musical area. During the years 1975 through 1980, three albums released by Arista won *DownBeat*'s critics poll as Album of the Year: Cecil Taylor's *Silent Tongues*, recorded at Montreux at the '74 festival where Backer and Cuscuna began hatching their Arista plot; Anthony Braxton's *Creative Music Orchestra 1976*, and Air's *Air Lore*, a radical reconstruction of two compositions each by Scott Joplin and Jelly Roll Morton alongside one Threadgill original. "My biggest objection to the interpretation of ragtime," Threadgill told *The New York Times*, "is that it's too classical. That music was hot. It was breathing. Nowadays you hear people playing ragtime, and they sound like they're playing Chopin. I never heard any black music in my life that didn't have a hot strain in it somewhere." In *The Rolling Stone Record Guide*, Bob Blumenthal called *Air Lore* "unsurpassed as a statement of historical homage from the perspective of the frontiers." Two albums on Savoy, *The Changing Face of Harlem* and the five-LP monument *Charlie Parker: The Complete Savoy Sessions*, won Grammy Awards for Best Liner Notes (Porter was also nominated for Best Historical Album for his essential survey of the Ravens).

The executives were given an unusual amount of leeway; as long as they hit their budgets, they were allowed to take chances. "We rode the crest of that wave as long as we could," Cuscuna says, and for those years, jazz at Arista was the most prestigious part of the young company. Near the end of 1979, Davis, in a *Billboard* interview, analyzed what he called "a polarized jazz market" and pointed out the disparity between the artists praised by the press (Air and Braxton, presumably) and artists who "enjoy a wider audience." Backer left the label in 1980; the same year, Arista Novus released its last albums, and Braxton ended his Arista period with *For Two Pianos*. Arista's Savoy relationship didn't last much longer, but before it expired, a lot of exceptional two-fers

ARISTA RECORDS, INC.
ARISTA BUILDING
6 WEST 57 STREET
NEW YORK, N.Y. 10019
(212) 489-7400

June 29, 1979

Dear Press Friend:

Enclosed you will find a limited edition special sampler
of our contemporary jazz product featuring Jeff Lorber,
whose first Arista album Water Sign will be released in
mid-July, GRP's Roland Vazquez and Tom Brown and selections
from Novus' Blue Montreux album and Nexus album. Please
feel free to contact me if you need any additional information on any of these artists.

In September we will be releasing Blue Montreux part two
along with new albums by Michael Gregory Jackson, Anthony
Braxton, Larry Coryell, John Scofield, Baird Hersey and a
special album of rags, both old and new, by the very exciting
Air.

Best wishes,

Barbara Shelley
Associate Director/
National Publicity

came out, including *Shouters* (starring Gatemouth Moore and H-Bomb Ferguson), *The Black Swing Tradition* (Fletcher Henderson, Stuff Smith, Hot Lips Page), and second volumes of *Ladies Sing the Blues* and *Black California*.

The year Backer and Arista parted ways, the label released its second album by the Jeff Lorber Fusion, *Wizard Island*. The group's namesake keyboard player wrote eight of the nine tracks. The ninth was composed by a young saxophone player who'd recently come on board, Kenny Gorelick. The tune was called "Fusion Juice." Further away from Anthony Braxton, while still blowing into a reed instrument, one could not get.

SOME LIKE IT HOT

THE SUMMER OF 1977 IN NEW YORK CITY was especially brutal, with oppressive heat, a citywide power blackout, Son of Sam on a tabloid-obsessed murder spree, and the Mets on a path to losing nearly a hundred games. In late August, the Arista staff did what all sweltering New Yorkers were tempted to do: go to the beach. That year's convention was held at the landmark Hotel Del Coronado in San Diego, a Victorian beach resort that had stood on that spot since 1888, and during Hollywood's first golden era was a getaway for cinema luminaries like Errol Flynn, Clark Gable, and Charlie Chaplin. The Coronado stood in for Miami Beach in Billy Wilder's *Some Like It Hot*. It was on those sands that Tony Curtis extended his leg and sent a never-more-desirable Marilyn Monroe into a romance-spurring pratfall. Arista's gathering would be, like the clash between the menacing "Friends of Italian Opera" and Sweet Sue and Her Society Syncopators, a combination of music and mayhem.

Arista had quite a bit to celebrate, and Clive Davis made certain that all of the label's priorities were touched upon over the four-day event. Davis had gone on something of a buying binge: He signed the Kinks, who had come off a sales decline at RCA after a string of conceptual albums; the Grateful Dead, persuaded to hitch up with a record label when their attempt to go out on their own proved too administratively cumbersome; and the Alan Parsons Project, which wasn't a band, but a musical laboratory where Parsons brought together vocalists and musicians to perform the works that he and collaborator Eric Woolfson concocted. So far, all of those acquisitions were paying off. The Kinks' *Sleepwalker*, the Dead's *Terrapin Station*, and the Alan Parsons Project's *I Robot* were all giving Arista a solid presence in the rock world, and each act would be at the core of the label's roster through the next decade.

There were other new signings, including Donovan (an artist Davis had shepherded at Epic), Dickey Betts from the Allman Brothers Band, and the Dwight Twilley Band. It had been a toss-up whether Arista would draft Twilley or Tom Petty from Shelter Records; after consulting with his team, Davis decided to put Arista's chips on Twilley and his bandmate Phil Seymour. In hindsight, that doesn't look so good, but at the time, the Twilley Band was coming off a semi-hit single, "I'm on Fire," and their album *Sincerely* had been cheered by the rock press as a refreshing brand of rockabilly-tinged power pop.

And there was an entire subset of Arista rock albums that could loosely be called "progressive," an area that Davis and his A&R staff pursued with varying degrees of enthusiasm. According to Happy the Man's Frank Wyatt's website, Davis came up to them after a set and said, "Wow, I don't really understand this music. It's way above my head, but my head of A&R, Rick Chertoff, says you guys are incredible, and we should sign you. So welcome to Arista." In all fairness, the first Happy the Man album's tracks, all complex instrumentals, included "On Time as a Helix of Precious Laughs," "Stumpy Meets the Firecracker in Stencil Forest," and "Knee Bitten Nymphs in Limbo," so a certain level of confusion was to be expected. The label took a lot of chances with left-field, geograph-

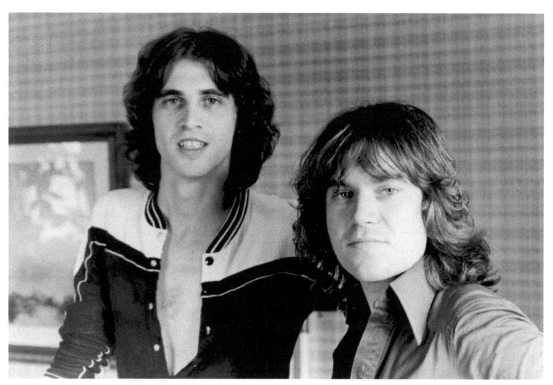

Dwight Twilley (left) and Phil Seymour.

Photo by Linda D. Robbins

ically diverse, arty rock: Japan's Stomu Yamashta (whose *Go Too* album featured vocals by Jess Roden and Linda Lewis); Pierre Moerlen's Gong, from France; the Italian prog rock band Nova; England's Camel; and David Sancious and Tone, whose leader, born in Asbury Park, New Jersey, had been the piano player in the E Street Band, but was now somewhere in the New Age ether.

As at the company's conclave in Arizona, the 1977 convention had live artist showcases. The Brooklyn-based funk outfit Mandrill, the New Commander Cody Band, and Aalon, a hotshot soul artist who'd done time in Eric Burdon's post-War band, played on opening night. The following evening was headlined by the Dwight Twilley Band, whose first LP for the label, *Twilley Don't Mind*, featuring (such was hoped) soon-to-be-hits "Looking for the Magic" (a snappy number with Tom Petty on guitar) and "Trying to Find My Baby," reached record stores a few weeks after this appearance. Davis and his PR and promo teams were gearing up for a big push. "Rock n' roll with all the sweat left in" was the way the album was marketed, as though the problem with other rock albums was insufficient perspiration.

Setting the stage for the Twilley Band was moody singer-songwriter Danny Peck, whose album debut, *Heart and Soul*, boasted an impressive cast of L.A.-based characters (David Paich, David Foster, Steve Lukather, Harvey Mason, the Porcaros...) but quickly slipped into obscurity. To wind things up on Saturday, Rick Danko, the first member of the Band to kick off a solo career after *The Last Waltz*, played songs from his Arista debut. And there was a set by a new band out of Los Angeles, the Pets (formerly called the Damaged Pets, after a Woody Allen stand-up routine).

The main songwriter and singer of the Pets was Gregg Sutton, who recalled in an interview in *Paraphilia*, "We were still selling the band to the people at Arista, which is just a fact of life when you're trying to make it. And we were trying to make it, which meant making it first with our own record company. And that record company, like any large group of people was filled with folks of every sexual proclivity. Thus, we thought it best

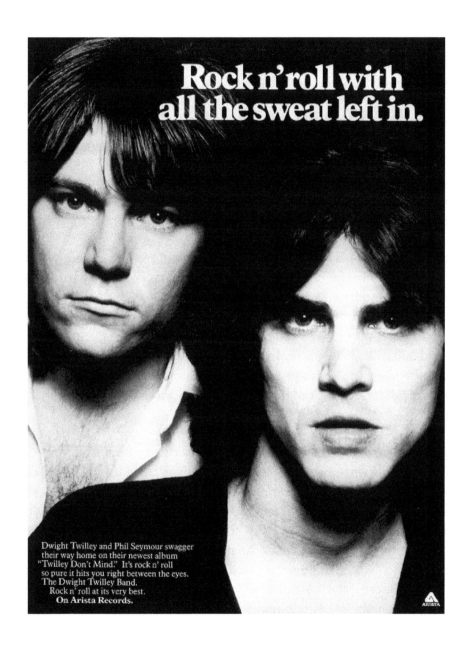

to maintain as much mystery as possible. Monogamy has its place but we didn't want it screwing up my career before it started." Arista had high hopes for the Pets. Sutton had been in the ill-fated "supergroup" KGB with Michael Bloomfield and Barry Goldberg, and the Pets were being handled by Lookout Management's Elliot Roberts (Joni Mitchell, Neil Young). Clive Davis, who saw them at a showcase at SIR in L.A. with his West Coast A&R guy Roger Birnbaum, was impressed by Sutton's songs, and would drop in the studio when he was in town to check on the album's progress. Sutton remembers Davis saying, "If you think this song is over by the third chorus, you're sadly mistaken, my friend. You must modulate." Although the band thought "Desperately" should be the first single from the album, *Wet Behind the Ears*, Arista went with "Same Old Fool."

The band was ready to play for the troops at the Del Coronado. There was, Sutton recalled, a copious amount of cocaine and Quaaludes ("I remember getting caught with Danko in a closet, and he was a very, very garrulous fellow, but he'd never look you in the eye"), a bass guitar that went missing (someone from Danko's crew went off with it; "he probably stole it by accident"), and a decent-enough set. But the album never took off, and Sutton is philosophical about it. "It was not how we intended it. We were supposed to be like a soul-infused Southern California sound. The basic tracks sort of reflected what we were doing, but things changed as we went along. But that's certainly not unique."

When the Arista employees and artists weren't huddling in closets and God knows where else, the staff was given two installments, over two afternoons, of previews of upcoming releases (*Record World* timed Davis's first presentation as a "five-and-a-half-hour session of listening," far from unusual) and new label associations. In his remarks to his staff, Davis claimed that Arista had "spiraled up with an unprecedented swiftness to claim its own major musical space." Arista had made a distribution deal with Buddah Records, which would bring artists including Gladys Knight and the Pips, Norman Connors, Melba Moore, Phyllis Hyman, and Andrea True (and, very briefly, Chic, whose contract became an object of contention between Buddah and Atlantic) into the Arista family, and a similar deal with Marty Scott's New Jersey-based Passport Records, which previously had been distributed by ABC Records. Buddah and Passport were brought on board to help Arista get more traction in, respectively, the R&B and rock areas. Mainstream R&B was always on Davis's mind, but Arista's ventures into that area—General Johnson, Martha Reeves, Bell holdover Lou Rawls, Shirley Brown (a promising singer who'd gotten some buzz on Stax), Garnet Mimms (a highly respected figure in the world of uptown soul from his records with Jerry Ragovoy)—weren't catching on. At the convention, Davis played cuts by up-and-comer Ray Parker Jr.'s group Raydio, whose "Jack and Jill" was on the verge of becoming a big R&B hit.

"I had this group called FM," Marty Scott says, "a Canadian trio which we had gotten a lot of good, coincidentally, FM airplay and sales on, and we had that on one of our other labels that we owned [Visa]. Clive liked all the airplay we had on their track 'Phasors on Stun,' and he wanted that. And we had Synergy, Larry Fast's *Electronic Realizations*, and this is right before I put Larry together with Peter Gabriel to form his band. Then I had this concept record, and he was very intrigued by this, called the *Intergalactic Touring Band*, which is about this group put together by the Vibra Corporation and sent off into space. I had Brand X, which was Phil Collins's fusion band, Anthony Phillips, who was the original guitar player in Genesis, and Pezband, a power pop band—I was the first person to use it as a marketing tool, the term 'power pop.' We sent out power pop soda cans."

What Scott brought to the party, at least in theory, was a credible rock presence. His Passport roster also included Long Island's Good Rats, who Scott calls "a rock'n'roll bar band, but like the biggest bar band; incredibly big in a couple of parts of the country. Here in the metropolitan area they were headliners, and in Detroit." Many of those acts were part of Davis's announcement of the Passport deal in San Diego. There was optimism that, in the vein of the Alan Parsons Project, the elaborate *Intergalactic Touring Band* extravaganza—with a cast of dozens, including Rod Argent, Meat Loaf, Clarence Clemons, Ben E. King, and Annie Haslam—would put together some sort of prog-rock/AOR/sci-fi coalition.

Scott says, "We did a promotion tour. I'm on a podium explaining the story and playing some of the songs, because the band didn't exist. The first place we did it was Studio 54, which is a bizarre place to have a promotional thing for a rock record, and we went to Chicago, L.A., Atlanta, and Texas. Stephan [Galfas, the producer] and I flew around the country with Arista promotion people, and we had Kevlar jackets made with the Vibra Corporation logo." But despite all the hoopla (*Billboard* called it a "sophisticated work of art," Meat Loaf notwithstanding), "It didn't sell as well as we had hoped, and that's because people thought it was a rip-off of *Star Wars*."

There had to have been an immense feeling of relief and vindication in Arista's ascension. By the third quarter of 1977, the label ranked tenth in *Billboard*'s analysis of chart performance, and by the end of the year, it was up to sixth, "the only corporation to register a solid jump in the fourth quarter." In dollar terms, Arista announced on the eve of the convention that revenues from the recently concluded fourth quarter of its fiscal year "reached $13,943,000, marking the largest single quarter in Arista's history, and representing a 120.8% increase over 1976 fourth quarter net revenues." In April, *The New York Times* had run a long, splashy article by Geoffrey Stokes called "Clive's Comeback." The newspaper of record, the publication that Davis knew everybody read and respected, went into minute detail about his fall and rise, about how he turned a "once minuscule company" into "the industry's sixth-largest in less than three years."

Davis, in San Diego, ticked off all these impressive stats and cued up new music by Gil Scott-Heron, the Alpha Band, Manilow, the Dead, and the Muppets. He touted the soundtracks from *Close Encounters of the Third Kind* and *The Greatest* (there was a muddled inspirational anthem sung by George Benson on that one, called "The Greatest Love of All," that was off to a promising start at radio).

But one key artist whose music wasn't quite ready was Patti Smith. While on tour in May 1976 promoting her second album, *Radio Ethiopia*, Smith took a tumble from a Tampa, Florida, stage in the midst of singing "Ain't It Strange." Her injury (broken vertebrae in her neck) kept her on the sidelines for about a year, but she was back in the studio in

'77 working on the album that would become *Easter* with producer Jimmy Iovine. Also toiling away at the Record Plant in Manhattan was Bruce Springsteen, working on the legally stymied, long-delayed follow-up to *Born to Run*. As was his custom, Springsteen wrote and began recording far more songs than he had any intention of using on his album, and Iovine, who was engineering the Springsteen sessions, bouncing from room to room at the Record Plant, thought one song, "Because the Night," might be right for Smith. Springsteen gave his okay, and Iovine gave Smith a cassette, but it took her a while to get around to listening to it. She was, justifiably, somewhat skittish about doing a Springsteen song. The album she was making already had some terrific new songs: "25th Floor," "Till Victory," "Ghost Dance." But one night—she has told this story often—she was home waiting for her guy, Fred Smith, to call, popped in Springsteen's tape, and started writing her own lyrics. "Love is a ring, the telephone," one line went.

"Bruce wrote a couple of songs for Patti," Lenny Kaye says, "a little bit in our style, and we heard them—and I'm sure the tape has gone to tape heaven—but we said, 'Oh, it's like the stuff we do.'" Then "Because the Night" came in the door. "She played it for me over the phone, and the chorus is one of the great choruses of our time, and we were like, this is a great song, but it was about a guy coming home from work, working in the hot sun, whatever it was, and she transformed it. It's an example of what I believe is a true collaboration. It's not a cover, it's really like both of their sensibilities in one place through the miracle of chance."

As Smith and her group continued preparing for the unveiling of *Easter*, Arista was about to celebrate its third anniversary. *Billboard* published a multi-page supplement honoring the label in its November 26 issue, chock-full of ads, accolades and interviews with its executive team. New York mayor Abe Beame (who'd been name-checked for his economic "Big Mac scheme" in Loudon Wainwright III's "Talking Big Apple '75," but apparently held no grudge) wrote a letter stating, "The fact that you have concentrated on recording and promoting New York-born and New York-based artists such as Barry Manilow, Melissa Manchester, Patti Smith, and Lou Reed is another indication of your pride and faith in our

City." There was a full page of portraits of Arista's executive team (25 people: 21 white males, one female, just saying). There were tributes from Jann Wenner of *Rolling Stone* and A&R giant John Hammond. Patti Smith took out an ad thanking the label's president: "Thru him our work has telescoped/he has allowed us to survive w/music and principles intact," it read in part. Lou Reed's ad was more succinct: "Thanks a lot."

The proud three-year-old was celebrated with a blowout extravaganza at Studio 54, the oh-so-selective disco that opened in April '77 at 254 West 54th Street. Party-throwing was, to Clive Davis, an art, like recording, mixing, and sequencing an album or rehearsing, lighting, and staging a concert. Putting together a guest list was like casting a play. The Studio 54 shindig was a cavalcade of Manhattan cultural life in 1977. Attendees included two stars of Woody Allen's New York love story *Annie Hall*, Shelley Duvall and Paul Simon (did Simon, as he was out on the dance floor, realize that Arista was sitting on all those Jerry Landis and Tico and the Triumphs master tapes?); screenwriter Buck Henry, who came straight from hosting an episode of *Saturday Night Live*; photographer Francesco Scavullo; Arista and Columbia Pictures executives; and Arista artists Patti Smith, Al Stewart, Barry Manilow, Lou Reed, and Loudon Wainwright III. There were, respectively, roller-skaters representing the Bay City Rollers, a candelabra acknowledging Manilow as the Liberace of the Me Decade, bikers and robots in honor of the Grateful Dead (forgetting all about Altamont, apparently) and the Alan Parsons Project. One can assume that there were many people, in many nooks in the club, paying private tribute to the Kinks.

On the night before New Year's Eve 1977, the Patti Smith Group, now back in action (they'd played a gig the previous month in New York's Hayden Planetarium), took the stage at the short-lived CBGB's Theater on Second Avenue, the former site of the Anderson Theatre, a downtown venue of some importance before Bill Graham opened up the Fillmore East nearby. It was Smith's 31st birthday. The set, opening with the Velvet Underground's "We're Gonna Have a Real Good Time Together," featured a take on the Ronettes' "Be My Baby" and a half-dozen songs that would, in due time, appear on *Easter.*

One of those songs was "Because the Night," and its co-author, Bruce Springsteen, came out to join her and the group, a surprise in a couple of ways. First, Springsteen had been in his bunker agonizing over *Darkness on the Edge of Town* and hadn't done a live gig since August. (The following night, he popped up in Jersey to do some songs with Southside Johnny and the Asbury Jukes). Second, "Because the Night." It was a song that sounded instantly inevitable, something so perfect for Patti Smith, yet so recognizably Bruce Springsteen, and shockingly commercial. It was the holiday break, and not many Arista people were at the show, but a few fans from the label did turn out, including Andy McKaie and Melani Rogers from the label's publicity department ("I went backstage to give her a gift," Rogers recalls, "an Asian blouse in black satin"). When they got back to the office on January 2, they passed along the word that everyone should be prepared for a hit single from Patti Smith. "It was one of two things Patti always wanted," Rogers says. "That, and sitting on the couch and talking with Johnny Carson on *The Tonight Show*."

"Because the Night" saw the light of day in March 1978, and if there is one track, 200 seconds of music, that is the platonic ideal of the Arista single, this would be it. It's rock and pop, polished and urgent, dramatic and catchy. It had some of the melodrama of Shadow Morton's productions of the Shangri-La's (and Smith's voice bore some resemblance to the yearning throb of Mary Weiss). Without giving up an inch of her autonomy, without singing an "outside song" (Smith had always peppered her sets with covers, from "Mack the Knife" to the Marvelettes, and would occasionally toss them onto B-sides), she, Iovine, and her band achieved something Clive Davis must have longed for when he signed her, a genuine breakthrough, consistent with how she wanted to be perceived. To this day, Lenny Kaye says, "We're proud to play it. I mean, Bruce did give it its hook and its sensibility, but I know Bruce's demo, it's got a nice little Latin sashay to it, but we made it a rock song and with no apologies."

Arista sales exec Jim Cawley recalls, "It was a fascinating situation. What I remember about 'Because the Night' is two markets in particular that jumped out, Philadelphia and

Boston. The big Top 40 station in Boston, WRKO, added the record, and because Boston is Boston, and you have all those people who love progressive music, it really struck a note. You had it on the Top 40 station and you had tremendous airplay on WBCN, the rock station. In Philadelphia, you had WFIL, the big Top 40 station, and also you had WMMR, WYSP. That was such an incredible experience, because I was able to speak constantly to the two marketing managers and find out what was going on. What you yearned for at Arista were things like Patti Smith, which came to fruition with 'Because the Night.' It was as cool as anything."

"I was at Jimmy Iovine's 40th birthday party," Arista's Abbey Konowitch says, "and Bruce spoke. He said, 'It's unbelievable that Jimmy convinced me it wasn't that special, and I didn't need it. And not only did he give it to Patti Smith, but he let her change some of the lyrics, so she got some of my publishing.'"

It got her added to the playlist at powerhouse pop station WABC-AM in New York; *Easter* became a Top 20 album; Annie Leibovitz shot her for the cover of *Rolling Stone*; and Arista threw her a party at Max's Kansas City where, true to form, she concluded her performance by jumping on the tables and kicking around glasses and silverware. Barry Taylor and Alan Wolmark reported on the festivities for their *New Wave News* column in *Record World*: "Patti went berserk and it was a joy to see. ...The band was better than we've ever heard them, Patti looked more magnificently grotesque than ever, and the evening of good food and music ended splendidly with an incomparable rendition of the now-standard 'You Light Up My Life.'"

(The soundtrack album of *You Light Up My Life*—which didn't feature Debby Boone's blockbuster hit, but the original film version by Kacey Cisyk—had been released on Arista the year before, reconnecting the label with its composer Joe Brooks, and a sordid tale that is. Under the name Joey Brooks, he recorded a single for the Bell-distributed Aurora label; then, on Bell, he wrote and produced some sides for the young actor Robby Benson. In the *very* early months of Arista—catalog #AS-0100, to be

exact—the label released the Benson-Brooks collaboration "A Rock 'n' Roll Song" backed with "Messin' Up the Mind of a Young Girl." It came to light years later that Brooks was a serial sexual predator, and he committed suicide before his trial for 91 counts of rape and other sex crimes. He could never be charged for his musical crimes, like "Messin' Up the Mind of a Young Girl.")

Street Hassle, Lou Reed's second Arista album, came out in early 1978, weeks before *Easter*. Like *Easter*, it had a Springsteen component: Bruce did a spoken-word passage on the epic title cut, and the critical consensus was that it was Reed's best album since whatever the critic thought his last best album was. Since most reviewers agreed that his previous album, *Rock and Roll Heart*, had been less than inspired, there was a sigh of relief at Arista when *Street Hassle* chalked up kudos. Reed was trumpeting the "binaural recording" technique that he and co-producer Richard Robinson used, placing two mics in the studio to get a truer stereo sound, or something like that. It's unlikely that many writers got the full binaural experience (headphones recommended), but they responded to how engaged and purposeful Reed sounded, how very Reed-ian songs like "Dirt," "Leave Me Alone," the three-section "Street Hassle" opus, and the Velvet Underground's "Real Good Time Together" were. And Reed committed his, call it Norman Maileresque, "I Wanna Be Black," to LP and cassette.

It was a logical move, after *Street Hassle* put Reed back in the conversation, to record a live album that included some of his repertoire from the Velvet Underground and his solo years at RCA. It was the golden age of the double-live LP (in '78 alone, there were such documents by Ted Nugent, Little Feat, David Bowie, the Outlaws, Kansas, and Bob Marley and the Wailers, all trying to replicate the sensation that was *Frampton Comes Alive!*), and why shouldn't Arista have versions of "Sweet Jane" and "Walk on the Wild Side" in its catalog?

Was this necessary? Perhaps not. In the '70s, there had already been two live Velvet Underground albums and two live Reed albums—*Rock and Roll Animal* and *Lou Reed Live* (both taped at the Academy of Music in '73)—so how many variations on "Sweet

Jane," "Pale Blue Eyes," "I'm Waiting for My Man," and "Satellite of Love" did anyone need? Redundancy be damned, it was decided to capture Reed during a run of shows at the Bottom Line in May. Even for him, he was in a cantankerous, combative mood. He went off on tangents, sniped at adversaries real and imagined, and used his songs as premises for extended exegeses. In breaks from venting, Reed and his band did intense, focused takes on "Pale Blue Eyes," "Coney Island Baby," and numbers from *Street Hassle*. *Live: Take No Prisoners*, released in November '78, is, like Phil Ochs' *Gunfight at Carnegie Hall* and the Stooges' *Metallic K.O.*, the live album as confrontation. Reed uses "I Wanna Be Black," "I'm Waiting for My Man," and "Walk on the Wild Side" as reference points, but in this context you could hardly call them "songs." *Live: Take No Prisoners* has been called Reed's "comedy album," and his snappish NYC-hipster delivery is a little reminiscent of Lenny Bruce's. Some of his monologues have the cadence of beat poetry, but mostly they're like the unleashed spritz of Catskills comics at a Friars Club roast.

With a kind of sardonic glee in his voice—like, *I have the mic now, motherfucker*—he suggests that *Village Voice* writer Robert Christgau might be a "toe-fucker" and mocks *New York Times* critic John Rockwell for bringing a bodyguard to CBGB. He'd been particularly ticked off at Christgau for the B-plus grade the critic gave *Street Hassle* ("maybe he's better off not aiming for masterpieces"). Months later, at the Bottom Line, that still stung. "Can you imagine working for a fucking year and you got a B-plus from an asshole in the *Village Voice*?" This Festivus-like airing of grievances comes in the middle of what is ostensibly "Walk on the Wild Side" but is "Walk on the Wild Side: The Annotated Version." He lets his band carry the riff through most of the nearly seventeen minutes while he acknowledges Bruce Springsteen in the audience (this has now become a Vegas act with in-house celebrities), explains who the characters in "Wild Side" are ("Little Joe was an idiot"), and tells how producers approached him to write songs for an Off-Broadway musical based on the Nelson Algren book.

"I do Lou Reed better than anybody," he says at one point, striking a pose, and that's what makes this artifact so compelling. In the second half of the '70s, New York City was bursting with bands that were the spiritual descendants of the Velvet Underground: the Ramones, the Patti Smith Group, Blondie, Television, Talking Heads. Was Reed going to be pushed aside by upstarts like Elvis Costello, who won 1978's *Village Voice* critics' poll in a walk?

For a moment, it looked as though Elvis Costello, in fact, might become an Arista artist. Import copies of *My Aim Is True* were making their way to America, and the album was getting a lot of press raves. Clive Davis was on the case, but he was not lacking competitors. It was complicated; Costello was on Stiff Records in the U.K., and Stiff was fielding offers from eager U.S. partners, but the two principals of Stiff, Jake Riviera and Dave Robinson, were not totally in sync about what the American move should be. Would Elvis Costello be part of a U.S. Stiff deal? As it turned out, nope. Riviera and Robinson were up to something that would split the Stiff roster. One U.S. A&R guy who was extremely impressed by Costello and *My Aim Is True* was Columbia's Gregg Geller, who'd been at the CBS Records convention in London when Costello decided to seek the attention of the label's personnel by busking outside the hotel they were staying at, getting arrested for his troubles.

Geller says, "In those days I was in London relatively frequently, and I would always return with a stack of records. And this time I probably brought back thirty LPs and a whole bunch of singles home with me, and at the top of the stack was the Elvis Costello album, which had just recently been released. I couldn't stop playing it." Geller contacted Brian Rohan, the attorney who was representing Costello's interests in the U.S. "I had no sense that there was any discussion of a total Stiff label deal." Then Geller was asked by one of the higher-ups at CBS International to go to Paris to check out a disco artist named Cerrone, and he decided "as long as I was going to Paris, I should also go to London to meet Jake Riviera. At that point, Jake was sharing an apartment with Nick Lowe, and I took a cab over, and I remember walking up some steps, and the door was open, and he was speaking to someone [on the phone] and saying, 'Gregg Geller from Columbia Records is here to sign Elvis.'

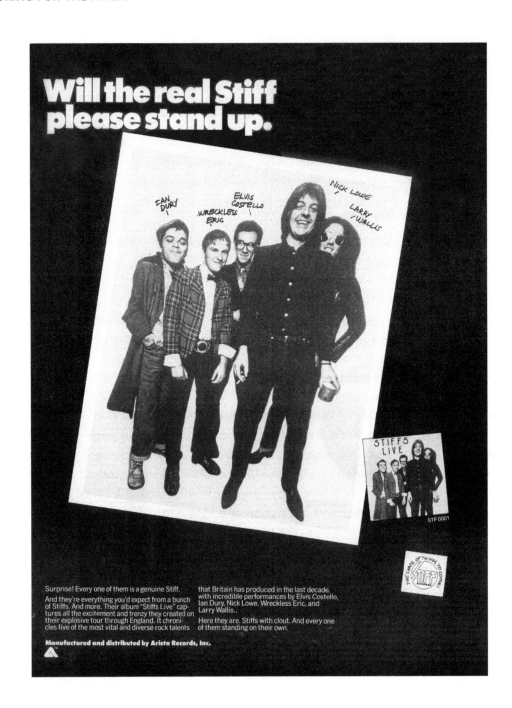

"When he hung up, he explained it was Clive Davis on the line, and when he told him that I had arrived, his response was 'Why would you sign with Gregg Geller? I hired him to work in the mailroom.' As far as Jake was concerned, that was terrific. I've always felt that Clive kind of cinched the deal."

On that trip, Geller also signed Nick Lowe after hearing a mix of "I Love the Sound of Breaking Glass." In the Riviera-Robinson divorce, Robinson kept the Stiff label and the rest of the Stiff roster, and Arista did the U.S. distribution deal with Stiff, probably guessing that any label shrewd enough to spot Costello and Lowe was likely to come up with even more intriguing talent. Announcing the alliance with an ad, "America Gets Stiff"—Florida, on the U.S. map, is in a state of arousal—Arista released two Stiff albums, Ian Dury and the Blockheads' *New Boots and Panties!!* and *Live Stiffs*, a compilation from a Stiff tour with tracks by Elvis Costello and the Attractions, Nick Lowe's Last Chicken in the Shop, Wreckless Eric, Larry Wallis' Psychedelic Rowdies, and Dury's group. Reviewers dug Dury's brand of hooligan-pub-rock: when the results were tallied in the aforementioned year-end *Village Voice* poll, *New Boots and Panties!!* just edged out *Easter* (*Street Hassle* also ranked in the Top 30). But compared to Costello, who was only 10 percent more nerdy and gawky than your standard-issue rock star, like one pulled off the factory floor only a step or two too soon, and armed with bracing, pointed songs, Dury was too genuinely odd to connect with U.S. audiences. Arista thought it would be a good idea to send him on the road with Lou Reed, and it really wasn't. There was, from all reports, mutual disdain between the two Arista acts. Dury said of Reed, "Fuckin' joke. He was about as subversive as a packet of chips." Which would have been a hell of a burn if anyone in America knew what a "packet of chips" was.

The whole Stiff–Arista pact imploded. Although there were periodic reports of forthcoming items like a Wreckless Eric album, nothing further showed up, and Stiff made a new arrangement with CBS. Trying to get the scoop on what happened, *Billboard* reported that it was "a severance neither party seems willing to discuss."

R&B BEST BETS

ALS 05

SIDE ONE

Jack & Jill
Raydio
From ARISTA AB 4163

Is This A Love Thing
Raydio
From ARISTA AB 4163

What It Is
Garnet Mimms
From ARISTA AB 4153

Johnny Porter
Garnet Mimms
From ARISTA AB 4153

How's Your Love Life
Eddie Kendricks
From ARISTA AB 4170

Where There's Smoke
Eddie Kendricks
From ARISTA AB 4170

SIDE TWO

Pack Up Your Bags
Harvey Mason
From ARISTA AB 4157

What's Goin' On
Harvey Mason
From ARISTA AB 4157

Straight From the Gate
Headhunters
From ARISTA AB 4146

Got To Give It Up
Pharoah Sanders
From ARISTA AB 4161

Answer Me My Love
Pharoah Sanders
From ARISTA AB 4161

ARISTA™

Arista had struggled a bit to get traction in R&B, but as Davis predicted in his San Diego product presentation, that was about to change. *Record World* magazine went along with the premise with an August 1977 article pronouncing "Arista Is Primed for an R&B Explosion." There was excitement surrounding the signing of Eddie Kendricks and Mandrill, each of whom came with a track record, and still-flickering hopes of getting hits with General Johnson and Linda Lewis (half of her second Arista album was recorded in New Orleans with producer Allen Toussaint, but *Woman Overboard* never got released in the U.S.). The dark horse in this contest was a new group called Raydio, formed by and named after Ray Parker Jr., an in-demand session guitarist and sideman for Stevie Wonder and Barry White. He'd also co-written the Rufus hit "You Got the Love" with Chaka Khan. He produced, wrote, sang, engineered, mixed, and played guitar on the debut album, *Raydio*. He was a genuine soul auteur, and his music was playful and sexual: he was a mild-mannered love man, quietly persuasive.

"Clive really wanted to go into R&B," Jim Cawley says. "We had some successes with R&B, nothing really big. We tried. Washington, D.C., was the most fertile market in the country to sell R&B, so along comes the Raydio album; it was the most thrilling experience ever. The distributor was tremendous in Washington. We went around before the album came out, and we played it for people. Within weeks, it was number-one in Washington, bigger than Parliament-Funkadelic, Earth, Wind and Fire, anything... There's nothing in the world like being able to make that phone call to Clive and say, 'I have news. Raydio, number-one at Soul Shack, number-one at Waxy Maxie, biggest retailer in D.C.' Those retailers didn't have much of a track record with us. Raydio changed everything."

Raydio pried open the door for what was called, in the trades, urban music, and Arista signed another young artist, a hotshot kid from Plainfield, New Jersey, who'd become a featured singer and player in the P-Funk universe. Glenn Goins was only 23 when he, along with some other members of George Clinton's musical organization, decided to jump ship (in the documentary *One Nation Under a Groove*, it's alleged that, at the end

RAYDIO.
Powerful enough to start at the top.

Raydio has a history that includes over a million hits.

Ray Parker, Jr. is only 23, but over the last 13 years he's been a major contributor to Marvin Gaye, Stevie Wonder, Seals and Crofts and Bobby Womack who have recorded with him and performed his material.

Ray has put together a group so exceptional they already have a hit single "Jack and Jill" that's crossing over and climbing up the charts fast.

Raydio. This group's so hot, they're starting at the top.

AB 4163

RAYDIO. THIS YEAR YOU'LL SPELL IT OUR WAY.

R&B: Billboard *7	Record World *5
POP: Billboard *48	Record World *34

On Arista Records and Tapes

of a tour, band members found their paychecks had been woefully slim because Clinton deducted the cost of the drugs he provided on the road). About Goins's departure, Tom Vickers, P-Funk's Minister of Information, says Goins was "such a powerful vocalist and creative center of Parliament-Funkadelic during their glory days that it was really a shock, and you could feel the air starting to go out of the P-Funk balloon."

Vickers continues, "There were at least three songs in the show that he was the dominant vocalist [on], and then, if you watch the Houston Summit show from 1976 on YouTube, he was the one who would do this sort of gospel-inflected 'I see the Mothership!' segment of the show, which was about five minutes from the time George would leave the stage to the time he would reappear coming out of the Mothership."

Davis had hired a new urban A&R guy, Vernon Gibbs, a music journalist (he'd profiled Gil Scott-Heron for *Playboy*) who had recently worked at Mercury Records. "When I got to Arista," Gibbs says, "the first deal I remember working on of any significance was [with] Robert Mittleman, he was associated with Parliament-Funkadelic, somehow he got Glenn Goins to sign with his management company, and I knew him from being around Parliament-Funkadelic, writing about 'em, and he brought the deal to me. Glenn was like a Sly Stone, and Clive actually saw him as becoming another Sly Stone. Mittleman played demos, and Clive made the decision to sign Glenn. So that was really my first shot at being involved with something that was hot."

What was intended as only the first of many Glenn Goins projects for Arista was a group called Quazar, fronted by Glenn's younger brother Kevin but with Glenn's fingerprints all over it. In addition to producing the album, Glenn co-wrote (sometimes with fellow P-Funk mutineer Jerome Brailey) more than half the tracks, played some guitar, bass, and drums, did some vocals. It was an edgy, exuberant album, absolutely of its moment, really hammering home the whole funk situation. Its first three tracks are "Funk With a Big Foot," "Funk With a Capital 'G'" (Goins, we can surmise), and the leadoff single, "Funk 'n' Roll (Dancin' in the Funkshine)." The 45 was scheduled for release in August.

In July, Glenn passed away, felled by Hodgkin's lymphoma. "The album was finished," Gibbs says, "and he was starting to work on his own album." Goins was 24 years old.

"As a songwriter, as a vocalist, as a guitarist and as a frontman," Vickers says, "he could do all of the above at a very high level of showmanship and artistry. He was the real deal, you know, and anybody and everybody who saw that show would just walk away, like jaw on the ground about this guy Glenn Goins. I mean, he was that talented."

A second Arista album from the P-Funk family came from another New Jerseyan, keyboard virtuoso Bernie Worrell. But unlike Goins, who severed ties with Clinton and that whole crew, Worrell had the endorsement and participation of his former employer. *All the Woo in the World* was co-produced by Worrell and Clinton and features an impressive lineup, including horn players Fred Wesley and Maceo Parker. The album was "Produced & Designed With Your Woo in Mind," which was very considerate of everyone involved. Talking to *Blues & Soul* magazine, Worrell said, "It isn't really what people would expect … The music for the album isn't in one special vein—there's a bit of jazz, a bit of funk, avant-garde, and even a shade of classical music." It is possible, at that point, that the Clinton contingent was getting spread a little too thin, and Worrell's album got lost. "Bootsy blew up so big," Vickers says, "and Parliament and Funkadelic were so big that every major label—and minor label, for that matter—wanted a piece of that P-Funk energy and music and vibe George was creating." Of course, Arista wanted some of that action, but Goins's death made promoting Quazar a challenge, and despite the splendid idea of "Insurance Man for the Funk" (who wouldn't take out one of those policies?), fans weren't ready to add all that woo to their P-Funk libraries. Both *Quazar* and *All the Woo in the World*, however, have seen major bumps in their reputations in the secondary funk market.

It wasn't quite the R&B "explosion" that *Record World* and Davis had predicted in the summer of 1977. There were excellent performances on Eddie Kendricks's album *Vintage '78* (it was a smart move to have him cover David Forman's "If It Takes All Night" and turn it into a swoon-worthy falsetto come-on), but it was a tough time, with disco still the primary musical pulse, for classic soul. Arista tried to split the difference between soul and dance music with General Johnson's "Can't Nobody Love Me Like You Do," Garnet Mimms's "Right Here in the Palm of My Hand," and Mandrill's "Happy Beat" and experimented with Barry White-inspired boudoir-soul with swamp-rocker Tony Joe White ("We'll Live on Love"). Linda Lewis's album stayed on the shelf when the Tony Macauley-written-and-produced single "Can't We Just Sit Down and Talk It Over" didn't generate any heat. There was an ad campaign, "What's happening on the street?" that positioned Arista as a hotbed of R&B activity, spotlighting Kendricks, Mimms, Mandrill, and Raydio, along with other Arista (and Buddah) artists like Harvey Mason, Melba Moore, and Gene Page (who put out dance-conscious renditions of the themes from *Close Encounters of the Third Kind* and *Star Trek*, as well as the "Moonglow/Love Theme" medley made famous in the 1955 movie *Picnic*, because there was no melody on the planet that could not be disco-accessorized). The ad was more aspirational than grounded in what was actually "happening."

Near the end of 1978, Davis made an agreement to distribute a newly formed label, one that provided the commercial-jazz solution he'd been looking for, with an R&B kicker. GRP Records, headed up by Dave Grusin and Larry Rosen, specialized in swirling, pulsating city music, most of it from the boroughs outside of Manhattan. Trumpeter Tom Browne was from Queens (his hit was "Funkin' for Jamaica (N.Y.)"), flautist Dave Valentin came from the Bronx, and vocalist Angela Bofill was born in Brooklyn and raised in the Bronx. While this music was not exactly in alignment with Steve Backer's own taste, in interviews he was philosophical: "GRP is producing LPs which are falling right in the pocket of what's occurring in fusion today. Many jazz purists frequently look down upon fusion, but if it weren't for the fusionists and the crossover artists, purists would not have the opportunity to record that they [have] today."

The first single from Bofill's debut album, *Angie*, was the midtempo ballad "This Time I'll Be Sweeter," the song that DeCoteaux and Silvester cut with Martha Reeves and Linda

Lewis for Arista. But most of the tracks on the album, including the highlight "Under the Moon and Over the Sky," were written by Bofill. She was a real discovery, an original. She was utterly modern and multicultural, but she was also sort of a throwback. There was jazz in her phrasing, and Latin pop in the arrangements, and some of the pre-rock sentimentality of the post-WWII era. You could imagine her in a film noir NYC nightclub, drawing attention away from whatever dark shenanigans are going on between the protagonists: who *is* that girl? Is it any wonder that Pete Hamill, the Bard of Brooklyn, fell under her spell? In his *New York Daily News* column he wrote, "The music was like a city dream ... I wish that all the city's windows would open at once, and we would hear this voice, loud and strong and lyrical, singing in a fresh new way."

EVERY SWITCH IS THROWN

WHEN CLIVE DAVIS WAS A GUEST on Tom Snyder's *Tomorrow* show in the fall of 1978, the abrasive host put the record executive on the grill, asking Davis to confirm a series of rumors about the label. "True or false," Snyder asked, "that Arista is up for sale?" "Absolutely untrue," Davis replied. Snyder asked whether Barry Manilow was responsible for keeping the label afloat, which gave Davis, a master of spin, the chance to rattle off a list of current and forthcoming projects that testified to the depth of the Arista roster. Still, that was an accusation, or from the point of view of the industry, an observation, that always colored a discussion about Arista: that without Manilow's steady stream of hits, and triple-platinum albums, the company would be struggling financially. As 1978 was heading into its holiday sales season, Arista was about to release a Manilow *Greatest Hits* album. (The most recent Top 10 single on the double-LP set was a version of Richard Kerr and Will Jennings' "Somewhere in the Night," which Davis had originally cut with a folk-pop duo, Batdorf and Rodney, back in '75: if he believed in a song, he was reluctant to shake it off.) But *Greatest Hits* would be the last time a Manilow album hit the triple-platinum mark, and he would have only two more Top 10 pop singles: a version of Ian Hunter's "Ships" and "I Made It Through the Rain," which was like "I Write the Songs" crossed with "My Way."

Manilow and his fellow Bell alumna Melissa Manchester, who went from being an aspiring Carole King or Laura Nyro to going Full Barbra on the histrionic "Don't Cry Out Loud" and the Hamlisch/Sager-penned theme from *Ice Castles*, were still part of the Arista lineup four years after "The New Record Company" was born at 1776 Broadway. So were Gil Scott-Heron (his 1978 album, *Secrets*, had his biggest R&B single, "Angel Dust"), the Breckers (with the live *Heavy Metal Be-Bop*), the Outlaws, and Braxton. But if Arista were to thrive as the '80s approached, it needed to break through with more artists.

In an odd twist, considering that they were regarded as probably the most "British" of the British Invasion bands—*Face to Face, Something Else, The Kinks Are the Village Green Preservation Society*, and *Arthur* are like guided tours of Ray Davies' Great Britain— the Kinks essentially became an American Band and had a major resurgence. From '78 through '80, you could hear Kinks songs everywhere. Van Halen made their entrance with "You Really Got Me," and the Pretenders debuted with "Stop Your Sobbing." The Jam cut "David Watts," and the Knack did "The Hard Way." (At the sessions for their third album, ex-Box Top Alex Chilton's band Big Star did "Till the End of the Day," but it stayed in the vaults for ages.) Hard rock, new wave, the mod revival, power pop, even punk (although Ray Davies took a cantankerous shot with "Prince of the Punks") all bowed in the direction of the Kinks. Meanwhile, the Davies brothers and their cohorts were moving toward mainstream AOR, spending most of their time in the U.S. (Ray had taken an apartment on the Upper West Side of Manhattan) and making their most "American" album, *Low Budget*, recorded at Manhattan's Power Station and Blue Rock Studios.

Released in the summer of 1979, *Low Budget* was riled-up rock'n'roll that was perfect for the political temperament, the "malaise" of the end of the Carter administration, the unease that came from the recession, hostages in Iran, long lines for gasoline, the decline in national self-esteem that directly led to the reign of Reagan. "Attitude," "(I Wish I Could Fly Like) Superman," "Misery," "A Gallon of Gas," and "Catch Me Now I'm Falling" all spoke

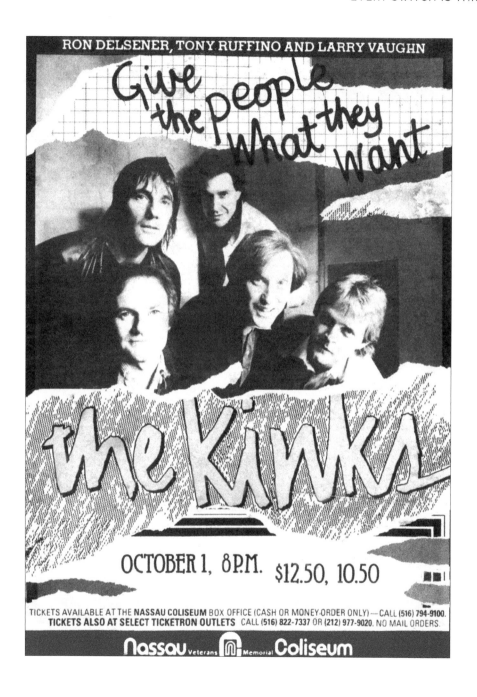

and rocked bluntly. It was music made for arenas, and if earlier Davies songs sounded as though they were deftly inscribed with a fountain pen, these were boldly scrawled with cans of spray paint. Where once he was resigned and wistful about the things that bugged him—if he was annoyed by snapshots taken on holiday in "People Take Pictures of Each Other," can you imagine what his response would be to sexting and selfies?—now he was venting quite loudly indeed: In a reverse of the Elvis Costello line, he used to be amused, but now he was disgusted. The shows from that era, like those documented on 1980's *One for the Road*, relied heavily on these anthems of aggravation, and where they dipped into the past, they mainly stuck to the theme: "Where Have All the Good Times Gone," "20th Century Man," "The Hard Way."

But the Kinks were still the Kinks, even as their Arista albums went gold. As the label's tour publicist, Jill Christiansen says, "I remember an incident out at Nassau Coliseum where the contingent came out from Arista, and something happened at the show, I think between Dave [Davies] and Mick [Avory], and Mick stormed off the stage. There was some issue, and I remember going into the dressing room and there'd been some kind of food fight with Indian food, and I had to come out and tell the Arista people, 'You can't come backstage.' The Kinks were covered in curry."

"We had a couple of limousines," Mike Bone, Arista's head of rock promotion, remembers. "We were going to go out to Nassau Coliseum to do the gold record presentation. Of course, there was Clive, Elliot Goldman, [promo VP Richard] Palmese, and for some reason I was in the car with Clive. The Kinks, of course they don't want to do anything prior to the show. They want to make sure that we stay for the whole fucking thing. Anyway, we're out in the crowd, and they get into a fight on stage. Everybody can see that they're arguing about something up there. The show is over, we go back to the hospitality room, and we got the gold records lined up. And the next thing you know, you hear stuff in the dressing room, voices yelling and screaming, things breaking. Their manager, Elliot Abbott, goes, 'Can you guys just mail us the gold records?' Clive was looking at his watch and flipping out."

There was another British rock act Arista was high on, Graham Parker and the Rumour. Other labels were lined up to woo Parker, and why not? His first two albums with the Rumour (veterans of Britain's vibrant pub-rock movement), released in the U.S. on Mercury Records, had critics doing effusive cartwheels, and when Parker extricated himself from that contract—complete with the lacerating kiss-off track "Mercury Poisoning"—a number of labels thought they could do a better job. When Arista won the bidding war, it was a kind of a coup, and when Parker delivered his first album for the label, 1979's streamlined blast of adrenaline that was *Squeezing Out Sparks*, produced by Jack Nitzsche, everyone was on board for what they were confident would be the major breakthrough, the type of about-time success that Springsteen had with *Born to Run* and Tom Petty would have later in the year with *Damn the Torpedoes*.

The lyrics lobbed like grenades: "There's nothing to hold on to when gravity betrays you," "You look all right in the cheap print dress," "All the odds are stacked against you," "Every bomb is detonated, every switch is thrown." And the shows around the time of the album, a bunch of them simulcast live on AOR stations across America, were stunning. The band started on the West Coast, playing the Roxy in Los Angeles and the Old Waldorf in San Francisco, and by the time they hit New York for shows at the Copacabana and the Palladium, they were un-toppable. Having the *Sparks* songs as the set list foundation helped, and Parker continued to dip into the soul catalog for covers: Ann Peebles' "I'm Gonna Tear Your Playhouse Down," the Trammps' "Hold Back the Night," the Jackson 5's "I Want You Back." Reviewing the Palladium gig for *The New York Times*, Robert Palmer praised the band's "unflagging intensity" and said, "The show was the sort on which reputations are made." Reputations, perhaps. Airplay and sales, somewhat less. At least not commensurate with Arista's hopes and expectations.

Arista stuck with Parker, clandestinely (initially) getting the heretofore "underground" "Mercury Poisoning" out into the world to grab some attention, releasing a single of "I Want You Back (Alive)," sending out promo items (little toy gizmos that squeezed out actual sparks). With the live GP&R shows getting so many stellar reviews, Arista's

head of publicity, Dennis Fine, and head of rock promotion, Scot Jackson, thought it'd be a fun idea to service press and radio with a promo-only album of all the songs from *Squeezing Out Sparks*, in sequence with a couple of bonus tracks, recorded live. The tracks on *Live Sparks*—the first time a complete live version of a studio album was released on the heels of the original—were taken from the April 9 Old Waldorf show that aired on KSAN and an April 28 show in Chicago broadcast on WXRT. It was a noble effort, and the studio *Sparks* did sell better than the Mercury LPs had. It was a vindication when the album—against such competition as the Clash's U.S. debut, Talking Heads'

Fear of Music, Neil Young's *Rust Never Sleeps*, and Elvis Costello's *Armed Forces*—was voted 1979's best (by a solid margin) in the *Village Voice*'s annual critics poll.

The relationship with Buddah Records took a quirky turn when Art Kass, the label's president, made a deal to distribute Ze Records, a new label devoted to the fringes of rock, pop, and dance music. Kass said at the time, "We were one of the major reasons for Arista to expand their disco department, and the Ze product will be an exciting addition." Ze was how James White and the Blacks, the Contortions, Don Armando's 2nd Avenue Rhumba Band, Lizzy Mercier Descloux, the Aural Exciters, Lydia Lunch, and Cristina wound up being distributed by Arista Records. On paper, a more screwball match-up of musical agendas one can't imagine. The music was abrasive at times, plain wacky at others: James White squalling on sax through "(Tropical) Heat Wave," the Aural Exciters taking the Millie Small hit "My Boy Lollipop" into surreal dance music/girl group territory, Cristina bouncing through August Darnell's "Blame It on Disco." It was tremendous fun, true underground music coming to the surface, and it was the brainchild of Michael Zilkha, who arrived in New York City after graduating university in England in 1975, immediately located CBGB, and dove straight into the madness.

"I came to New York wanting to write about music for the *Village Voice*," Zilkha says. "Music was my identity. I'd always idolized John Cale, I was just around that scene, and it was John Cale that started me in the record business. I went to interview him for *Interview* magazine and we became friends. I knew [Island Records head] Chris Blackwell, and I suggested to Chris he sign Talking Heads, and he didn't sign them, and he regretted that."

"Then I met August Darnell in a studio. He was recording James White and the Blacks, and that's the nexus of everything. Of the Arista albums, it's basically my relationship with August. He gave me a fabricated band initially, Don Armando's. He wasn't going to give me the crown jewels, Kid Creole and the Coconuts, which were a fantasy of his."

Ze wound up at Buddah because no one else would have it. "When you start a record label, not only does no one want to distribute you, no one wants to sign with you, either. Because you have no track record. Basically, you're going to sign people no one else wants. The label was so new, the Contortions didn't want to give me the Contortions, 'cause they didn't know what would happen. I said I'd rather have a disco band, and they said all right, you can have James White and His Blacks. I said, 'Well, I'd prefer James White and *the* Blacks.' As soon as we made the James White record, by then they were getting used to me, and they knew I wasn't frightened of anything. I wasn't going to dilute them. So immediately they gave me the Contortions as well."

James White was the front man of both bands—the Contortions were the "rock" band, the Blacks were the "jazz-funk-dance" band—and both liberally stretched those categories. As Richard Riegel wrote in *Creem*, "Whether you go with the 'rock' of *Buy the Contortions*, or the 'disco' of *Off White*, you may just find a musical summation of everything the punk revolution of 1976–1977 seemed to be aiming toward: pop muzik stripped of all melody and harmony and needless emotion (at least for the time being) to get back to the basics of rhythm."

"It was a deal where there was no advance," Zilkha says, "and Buddah had a huge debt to Arista. So they started putting out our records, and 'Deputy of Love' [by the Don Armando configuration] was a big hit. Number-one on the disco charts. I was owed money, but Buddah said they didn't have the money. Buddah was owned by Morris Levy, and he was the money. Tommy Mottola arranged a meeting with Morris Levy, and he offered me fifty cents on the dollar. I settled with Levy, and it was very, very scary. At the end of the meeting, I mentioned that, of course, this was a matter of principle. And he went apoplectic. He said, 'If it's principle, fuck you'."

Arista had formed a Disco department in April 1979 under the direction of Audrey Joseph, and Davis already sounded begrudging about the whole idea: "We certainly intend to pursue this direction further," he told *Billboard*, "but only part and parcel of being a diversified label and always with an ear for long-range artistry rather than the fabrication of immediate, disposable product." Translation: I'm not so sure about this. He was right to strike the cautious note; there were already signs of a disco backlash, and there was some discussion about the wisdom of releasing a single called "Disco Nights" by GQ, a new band Arista had signed. Vernon Gibbs and the new head of Arista's R&B A&R, Larkin Arnold, had gone to the Bronx to see GQ, a self-contained outfit previously known as the Rhythm Makers.

"We went up to the South Bronx in a cab," Gibbs says, "and went down to a basement and there were these four guys set up. The first song they did was 'Disco Nights.' I looked at Larkin and he looked at me and there was no question. It didn't matter what else they had. It didn't have a disco beat; it's not straight four-on-the-floor, and they could have easily called it 'Feeling's Right,' which is what they said to me at one point, because they realized that was probably going to be the last great disco record. They knew it, everyone knew that this was the end of the disco era. I didn't look at them as a disco group; I put them in the same class as Cameo, or even Earth, Wind and Fire, even though they didn't use horns."

As predicted, "Disco Nights (Rock-Freak)" (the subtitle was a way of hedging the disco bet) was a big hit: number-one R&B, number-three dance, nearly Top 10 pop. Working that record as an indie promo person was one thing that got Joseph the new position at Arista. And the new department did well with artists like Black Ivory (a Buddah act), Harvey Mason, and Angela Bofill's dancier things. "So we got 'Deputy of Love' to number-one," recalls Debbie Caponetta, who had been an assistant in the rock promotion department before moving over to do promo in the disco department. "And then right around when it went to number-one is when Clive decided to close the dance department, and Michael Zilkha decided to hire me at Ze." The Ze-Buddah-Arista association broke down. "I was on my own," Zilkha says, "which was fine, because I did deals with Sire, Geffen, and Island."

Patti Smith and Lou Reed each released a new album in the spring of 1979. There was a solo album by Dwight Twilley, and Arista's U.K. company had signed Iggy Pop, whose initial LP under the deal was *New Values* ("I'm bored," Iggy groaned, "I'm the chairman of the bored"). Someone had the notion to have the Outlaws cover Elvis Costello ("Miracle Man"). There were funky one-offs by Bobby Womack (*Road of Life*, partially recorded in Muscle Shoals) and the Ohio Players (*Everybody Up*). In July, the Kinks' *Low Budget* came out. That month, it was announced that an agreement was reached wherein Columbia Pictures would sell Arista to Ariola-Eurodisc, which was the music division of the West German company Bertelsmann. *Record World* reported that the price for Arista was $50 million, "the greater portion of which represents 'the repayment of Arista's indebtedness to Columbia,' according to a Columbia Pictures statement." The article went on to say that Arista would continue to be independently distributed, and that Clive Davis would remain under contract as president and chief executive, while getting a buyout of his 20 percent share of Arista stock.

SHINES AND BEAMS DOWN THE BACK ALLEY STREAMS

"Clive Davis has this disconcerting habit of buying me lunches when I don't even work for him. (I think.)" —Lester Bangs

THERE WAS A TIME, LONG AGO, before everyone with a keyboard and a Wi-Fi password felt compelled to weigh in on every pop culture event, when the music press had a real impact. There was a codependent relationship between record labels and rock writers, especially in the 1970s, when there was money to spend on lavish press parties, when the labels could pick up the food-and-drink tabs for critics at the Bottom Line, when concert tickets didn't cost the equivalent of a month's rent for a Queens studio apartment, and plus-ones were a given. Promo T-shirts and other nifty knickknacks were common (Sire Records sent out miniature Louisville Slugger black baseball bats to hype the Ramones). To a great extent, artists like Bruce Springsteen and Patti Smith were the beneficiaries of what some people called the East Coast Rock Critic Establishment (mostly New York writers, but publications like Boston's *Phoenix* and the *Real Paper* had weight as well). People read the *Village Voice*, *Creem* (based in Detroit, but album reviews were assigned out of New York by Billy Altman), *Trouser Press*, *Musician*, and *Rolling Stone*, Jay Cocks and Jim Miller in *Time* and *Newsweek*, and the writers for the local papers, especially *The New York Times*.

Clive Davis liberally used large-font quotes from rave reviews in his trade and consumer ads. He would get upset and fire off scolding letters when writers like Robert Hilburn in the *Los Angeles Times* took what Davis perceived as unwarranted shots at Arista artists' aesthetic value (surely, there should be room for "entertainers" in the scheme of things; it was a nagging issue when he thought a critic was being snobbish). And even though not every act on the Arista roster was a darling of the press, Arista's publicity department had, it seemed, unusually close ties to the musical Fourth Estate. Paul Nelson, album review editor at *Rolling Stone*, was in a relationship with Arista publicist Betsy Volck, and had a standing lunch date with Andy McKaie at La Strada, Nelson's favored midtown Italian joint, for veal piccata and two Coca-Colas. Lester Bangs would drop by the office a lot to grab a stash of Savoy and Freedom albums and corral someone to take him to lunch; he might suggest the Russian Tea Room, but would settle for Two Bears, a casual, less stuffy, spot on 56th Street. Or he would call and get Melani Rogers on the line. "He'd say, 'Let me just read something to you,' and I would say, 'Lester, I can't stay on the phone.' I was still the department secretary. Lester said, 'Just tell Dennis and Andy you're on with me.' And he would read to me whatever he was writing at the time."

Department head Dennis Fine was close with Jay Cocks. Billy Altman from *Creem* and Ira Robbins from *Trouser Press*, both graduates of the Bronx High School of Science, had friends in PR. Rogers had gone to college with James Spina, a writer for *Women's Wear Daily*, and when she started doing publicity, she got Spina to do a *WWD* story and photo layout on Patti Smith that also ran in *W* ("Patti was thrilled"). Everyone was out at shows, all the time, socializing, dating, sharing tips on artists to see. It was a professional life that very closely resembled a social life. It all blended together. There'd be trips out to My Father's Place in Roslyn to see shows like the A's (a Philadelphia power-punk band Chertoff signed) opening for the Ramones, or out to Nassau Coliseum, the Stone Pony, or Jones Beach. Over the years, Davis, and Arista U.K., drew from the writer ranks for A&R staff: Vernon Gibbs wrote for *Crawdaddy*, the *Voice*, and *Jet*; Michael Barackman contributed to *Circus* and *Phonograph Record* magazine; Bud Scoppa wrote for *Rolling Stone*, *Creem*, and *Phonograph Record*; Ben Edmonds was a *Creem* editor and *Rolling Stone* contributor. It was quite cozy. Rick Dobbis says, "The press really mattered. Not only from the standpoint of credibility, but from the standpoint of creating success and recognizing success and championing things that could be successful. It was a really important part of the music business at the time, because you had a lot of really thoughtful, interesting people writing serious stuff."

This was all very much on Davis's radar. He knew what grades Robert Christgau was giving Arista albums in his *Village Voice Consumer Guide*. He'd tell visitors to his office about some glowing review for an Arista artist by John Rockwell in the *Times*. He'd have the PR department circulate clip packages of every week's standout articles and reviews throughout the company, and in the Friday executive luncheon, he'd be sure to point out to the sales and promotion departments when press was "leading the way," and retail and radio were comparatively lagging. As much as he would drill down on album sales in local markets—often he'd hear about "scattered ones and twos," meaning small dots of purchases in some stores—and on why certain singles weren't being added to key radio stations, he would want to know which critics had committed to attending a showcase, or a listening party, and if *The New York Times* had assigned someone to cover it.

It was a time when music journalism had clout; a review by Greil Marcus or Dave Marsh might not move the sales needle much (Marsh, for example, gave a pretty glowing notice to David Forman's album in *Rolling Stone*, and a fat lot of good that did; you could fill volumes of scrapbooks with raves about the New York Dolls), but it could be an indicator that an artist was the real thing: Graham Parker's post-Mercury signing derby was almost purely an example of press consensus outweighing sales. And an endorsement of an unknown, unsigned artist by a major critic with a national platform could change that artist's life, literally overnight. That's what happened with Willie Nile in 1978.

Willie Nile was doing a semi-regular gig as an opening act at Kenny's Castaways, after shuffling down from Buffalo years before. "I'm on stage playing," Nile says, "It was twenty people in the room, and there's this guy in the third row with glasses, kind of a nerdy-looking guy. He was totally digging what I was doing; I used to jump off the stage, I would introduce imaginary players, because I couldn't afford a band. Anyway, I got off the stage, and Don Hill [from Kenny's] said, 'This is Robert Palmer from *The New York Times*.' Don had told him, 'You should come early.' Then Thursday night the paper came out, I read it, and it was like he was my guardian angel. It was a life-changing review. I thought, 'Wow, it's like right out of a movie.'"

This was Palmer's lede: "Willie Nile, who is at Kenny's Castaways on Bleecker Street through tomorrow night, is an original. Stumbling upon him, as the writer did on Tuesday night, can be quite an experience, the kind that makes the daily grind worthwhile. For not only is Mr. Nile original, but also, on the concededly sketchy basis of just one show, he would seem to be the most gifted songwriter to emerge from the New York folk scene in some while." The final section on Nile (the poor headliner had become an afterthought) read, "[H]e is an exceptional talent, and it is hard to imagine his remaining unknown and un-recorded very much longer."

The review appeared in the Friday edition of the *Times*, July 29, 1978. That night, Kenny's was packed. The following night, Clive Davis showed up, and he approached Nile. "A meeting was set up; he wanted me to come up to the office. I went with my guitar. Everybody was there: Dennis Fine, Richard Palmese, Bob Feiden. I had to put on a show. The thing is, what I had was an inner confidence. I'm not Jackie Wilson, you know, but I believed in my songs." Nile had a bunch of them ready to roll out: "Vagabond Moon," "It's All Over," "They'll Build a Statue of You." "Then I said, 'I have piano songs,' so we all walked to a small room, and when I played 'Across the River,' Palmese goes, 'That's the one,' and Clive and him were, 'There's our hit.'"

Other labels were interested. Gregg Geller, who'd snapped up Elvis Costello for Columbia, came around. But Nile was in Davis's A&R zone: an energetic performer, something of a wordsmith, a rocker-poet (Palmer name-checked Bob Dylan *and* Gene Vincent, and who wouldn't be intrigued by that?), already getting critical approval. You can imagine that Davis saw in Nile at least a little of what he saw when John Hammond walked Bruce Springsteen into his office at CBS. (Nile had also done an acoustic showcase for Hammond not long after moving to NYC, and Hammond told him, 'You know, you've got something. You need a little more seasoning, and besides, I've just signed this kid from New Jersey...") Arista locked the deal down, Nile went into the studio with Roy Halee (known for his work with Simon and Garfunkel, but Nile says he was excited to work with him because he'd engineered Lovin' Spoonful records), and the label put him in position to be the first breakthrough artist of the '80s on Arista. Even before *Willie Nile* was released, Davis took Nile on the road as his acoustic opening act when he did a speaking tour of East Coast colleges.

Everything was in alignment. Showcases were booked, advance notices were strong, Nile got approached to open some arena dates for the Who on one leg of their summer 1980 tour. The trades chimed in. Samuel Graham and Sam Sutherland's column *The Coast* in *Record World* was typical: "We were trying to describe this new album by a young musician named Willie Nile to a friend not long ago, and about all we were able to come up with was, 'You know, he's from that New York school.' While that's essentially a nebulous description, of course, there is more than a touch of the New Yorker in Nile's music: tough, undecorated rock, laced with the kind of influences (jangling guitars, Dylanesque vocal delivery, songs that owe a considerable debt to Buddy Holly and others) that have done a lot to revive rock's waning spirit in recent months." "Rock's waning spirit" was a key phrase.

Yet for all of the huzzahs, all the label enthusiasm, and all the opportunities, the album stalled on the charts in the mid-100s. It came out at an inopportune time, for rock in general, and for the New York school he belonged to. Around the same time, early

Willie Nile's first album.

THE LOS ANGELES TIMES · ROBERT HILBURN · FEBRUARY 19, 1980

"Willie Nile's inspiring debut album signals the arrival of a major new figure in rock 'n' roll.

"It is the kind of rare collection that reawakens you to the inspiring qualities of rock 'n' roll. The sparkle of the guitars in the opening seconds of the album moves you, physically and emotionally, the way the best rock has always done.

"Imagine the joy of hearing an album with nearly a dozen uplifting selections. Nile's music touches freshly on some universal issues and combines two sturdy strains of American rock: the vitality of '50s-flavored rockabilly and the lyric slant of Dylan-oriented folk.

"This LP is evidence that an important new figure has arrived."

THE NEW YORK TIMES · ROBERT PALMER · FEBRUARY 15, 1980

"To these ears, Willie Nile *is the most exciting debut album by a singer-songwriter in some time.*

"He's a confident singer and a masterful songwriter who's able to fit bright, vivid imagery into the tightest rock-and-roll song forms…The result is an album that crackles with electricity. It is hard-edged guitar rock and would be squarely in a new-wave mold except for the unusually broad range of the songs."

STEREO REVIEW · PAULETTE WEISS · MARCH 1980

"It is dazzling—at times vibrant and driving, at other times tender and melodic.

"To describe the album as rock 'n' roll laced with folk is about as accurate as describing a Rolls Royce Silver Cloud as a large car with four doors. Nile's music is like a big surprise package into which twenty-five years of rock history are crammed. Despite recognizable influences (Buddy Holly, The Stones, and a clutch of British popsters and American rockabillies), Willie Nile has an unquestionable originality.

"The scope and authority of Nile's songs is impressive. They have wit and passion and even disturbing personal images. Willie Nile has enough talent and vision to make me believe he might be the Great Rock Hope for the Eighties."

AB 4260   Produced and Engineered by Roy Halee.

WILLIE NILE

Willie Nile.
On Arista Records and Tapes.
ARISTA

'80, Arista put out an album, produced by Jimmy Iovine, by East Coast rocker-with-attitude D.L. Byron, *This Day and Age*, but it all sounded as though everyone was trying way too hard to come up with a hybrid of Costello's Attractions and Springsteen's E Street Band, with a dollop of Billy Joel (who joined Byron on a single-only remake of Joe South's "Down in the Boondocks"). Like Nile's Arista debut, it floundered around the album chart's lower half.

It was a doldrums period, right in between the New York scene of the mid-to-late-'70s and the burst of modern rock and giddy pop that defined the first half of the '80s, when a confluence of events—the birth of MTV and the tangent second British Invasion, the rise of alternative rock radio, the start of the New Music Seminar and CMJ (College Media Journal), the introduction of the compact disc, all erupting within a few frantic years—gave the record industry a much-needed B12 shot. Arista, like every other label, scrambled to look for the next hot thing and, more often than before, had to do its scouting outside of New York. The creative balance was shifting away from Manhattan, the way it had in the middle and late '60s, when the first British Invasion and the West Coast sounds of Los Angeles and San Francisco drastically altered the musical land-scape. Davis and his A&R team were looking south (snapping up Capricorn Records bands like the Allman Brothers, Dixie Dregs, and Sea Level to join the Outlaws on the Arista roster, but that genre was past its heyday), looking west to California, and—even more productively—mining for potential gold in the U.K.

It was Davis's routine to spend, on average, one week every month in L.A., setting up camp at the Beverly Hills Hotel. Eve Babitz, who captured Los Angeles better than any writer since Raymond Chandler, sums it up in one of her essays: "Like all truly great hotels on earth, the Beverly Hills is an unflinching masterpiece, better than any museum, shopping center, or the Paris Opera House." She continues, "The best thing to do is park your car along Crescent, just north of Sunset Boulevard, and then walk over to the back of the hotel, where an insane, luscious garden is always abloom, around what they call 'bungalows,' which are little pink houses you can rent for about a thousand dollars a second."

Bud Scoppa, who Davis hired as a West Coast A&R guy, says, "Whenever he'd come to L.A., I would go over to the bungalow armed with a big stack of cassettes. He had this stereo, and it was always ridiculously loud, and I just stacked my cassettes on the coffee table and then he would spend the next hour or two playing me stuff, and I could never get my cassettes into the stereo."

Scoppa had reason to believe it would be simple. He'd gotten the A&R gig partly by, as was Davis's process when considering A&R candidates, making a tape of "songs that were current, that in my mind could be hits. I remember I had Cheap Trick's 'I Want You to Want Me' on there." Once he was hired, he got a call from Davis. "I think it was the night before I was supposed to go to the office, which was in Century City at that point, he had heard about this L.A. power pop band called the Pop, and they were playing in, I don't know, Costa Mesa or something like that. I drove down there, I checked them out, and they're pretty good. So the first band I saw, Clive signed. It was that easy to sign a band that I liked, which probably set me off on the wrong foot."

The Pop—Davis had real misgivings about the band's name, since the idea was to get them played on non-pop (i.e., rock) radio—were part of an emerging L.A. scene that included bands like the Motels and, a little bit later, X, the Go-Go's, the Bangles, and the Blasters, and had made an independent album in 1977 with a snappy, mod sound and hooky songs like "Down on the Boulevard." They were stylistically like a midpoint between the Cars (Arista tried to snag them, but were outbid by Elektra), whose debut was a 1978 pop-rocket, and the Knack, whose "My Sharona" was one of those undeniable singles. (Well, sort of undeniable: Scoppa says, "They did a showcase for us and they covered Beatles tunes, and they had 'My Sharona.' They were really quite good, but there was something about Doug Fieger that bugged me. I don't know if they would have signed with Arista rather than Capitol, but I didn't push it enough.") By the time the Arista album *Go!* came out, the Pop came across, unfortunately, as also-rans. The *Los Angeles Times* wrote, "The Pop got caught in the reaction against 'power pop' stirred up by the success of the Knack."

Scoppa also convinced Davis to check out a band called the Bus Boys, fronted by brothers Brian and Kevin O'Neal. They were an African-American band playing rock'n'roll from an edgy, sardonic perspective (their debut album was called *Minimum Wage Rock & Roll*, and it had songs like "KKK," "There Goes the Neighborhood," and "Johnny Soul'd Out"). Scoppa reserved a booth in a packed Madame Wong's on Wilshire Boulevard, and he remembers Davis being "blown away by them." It was a bold signing, but it felt as though the timing might be right for a black, new wave-influenced rock band. (Brian O'Neal told *Creem*, "We're the first black band to get national prominence to accurately reflect an Anglo influence on pop music through black musicianship.") Robert Margouleff, who'd worked with Stevie Wonder and Devo, was brought on board to co-produce with the O'Neal brothers. "I remember during the sessions at RCA in Hollywood," Scoppa says, "I was thinking, 'This isn't as exciting as they are live,' which I suppose was a learning experience for me."

The album was released in 1980, and according to Scoppa, "Then Prince's *Dirty Mind* came out and pretty much blew it out of the water, a much more cutting-edge album than we were able to do." Whether it was having their thunder stolen by Prince, or just the systemic resistance to black artists on rock radio, the Bus Boys didn't manage to find an audience for *Minimum Wage Rock & Roll*, but they got a break two years later when they were featured in Eddie Murphy's film *48 Hrs.*, doing "New Shoes" (from their second Arista album, *American Worker*) and "(The Boys Are) Back in Town." It was a love match: Murphy took the band on his *Delirious* tour, and they were the musical guest when he went back to host *Saturday Night Live* in early 1983. But at the time, despite the marketing hook and positive reviews, they were a commercial misfire. So was an unhinged album by West Coast singer-songwriter Tonio K (through Irving Azoff's Full Moon Productions). There is nothing else in the Arista catalog quite like 1980's *Amerika (Cars, Guitars and Teenage Violence)*. It's like a rococo mash-up of Randy Newman, *Bat Out of Hell*, and the Mothers of Invention; the fact that it exists at all is cause to celebrate. In *The Washington Post*, Robert A. Hull called *Amerika* "a revolutionary burlesque."

It was a shaky time for the whole biz, those few years after blockbusters like *Saturday Night Fever* and *Grease* (1978 was the biggest year for vinyl sales ever), *Songs in the Key of Life*, and *Rumours*, when going triple platinum was still impressive but not all that rare (Stephen Holden, a writer for *The New York Times*, wrote a pulpy novel about the industry that came out in 1980 called *Triple Platinum*). Disco had simply collapsed from exhaustion. Was 1980 one of the most fatigued in rock music history? Arista, a year or so after the label was sold off to Ariola/Bertelsmann, was experiencing something of an identity crisis. Patti Smith was in the first year of nearly a decade-long absence; she moved to Detroit, where she lived a non-public life with her husband, Fred "Sonic" Smith, and their kids. Lou Reed released his last album for Arista, *Growing Up in Public*, in '80, then bolted back to RCA Records. The Grateful Dead turned in *Go to Heaven* to the label that same year, then took about seven years off from studio recording (Arista filled the Dead gap with a pair of live double albums, *Reckoning* and *Dead Set*).

There were always things to brag about. Dionne Warwick made a surprising comeback on Arista (*Dionne*) after slumping sales on Warner Bros., with an assist from Manilow and Ron Dante. "Barry said, 'You gotta help me on Dionne Warwick,'" Dante recalls. "That whole sound, if you listen, it's a Manilow record. I was in there working with Barry, day by day, making sure that Dionne sounded good. We even did backgrounds together, me and Dionne and Barry. Beautiful album. It should have been a Manilow album. I said to Barry, 'You gave away a number-one record, 'I'll Never Love This Way Again.' I said, 'This is a giveaway,' and two or three of those sides on the album could have been Manilow singles. I thought it was just a bad move, but Barry wanted to be a producer." It was the type of project Davis excelled at, and in Warwick—who knew how precarious success was, and was willing to trust—he found an artist he could make sound shiny and current, and get her back in the game.

The Kinks, bless their combative hearts, continued their '70s resurgence into the '80s. And Arista could rely on album sales from the Alan Parsons Project, based on... well, it's not easy to say. There was never a tour, television appearances, an identifiable vocal sound, or a standout instrumental focal point. *I Robot* could have easily been a one-off fluke. It wasn't as though the concepts, such as they were, of subsequent albums were that compelling. The whole Parsons mystique was about his résumé: he was an engineer at Abbey Road for the Beatles, the Hollies, Pink Floyd, and others, and then a producer (one of his albums with the band Pilot came out on Arista U.K.). The angle was that he and his cohort Eric Woolfson assembled a cast of singers and musicians in the studio to create these thematic works. Starting with the second Arista album, *Pyramid*, one of the occasional participants was Colin Blunstone, lead singer of the Zombies, who first met Parsons when the Zombies were recording *Odessey and Oracle* at Abbey Road.

"I think there was always an air of mystery about The Project," Blunstone says. "Alan and Eric kept the concept of the album very secret, and any casting process that went on was also very private." The first Parsons track Blunstone was featured on was *Pyramid*'s "The Eagle Will Rise Again." "I remember Eric Woolfson asking me what I thought 'The Eagle Will Rise Again' was about, and I didn't have a clue! The tracks were always more or less finished when I put my vocal on." Blunstone was only one of a rotating gang of singers on the Parsons albums. Pilot's David Paton took some leads (and played bass), Lenny Zakatek and Chris Rainbow did a bunch of others, and—more and more—Woolfson stepped up to the mic. Blunstone is missing from the misogynist debacle *Eve* and *The Turn of a Friendly Card*, but returned for what was the biggest APP LP, *Eye in the Sky*. "We nipped into an empty Studio 3," he recalls, "and Eric sat at the piano and played and sang 'Old and Wise.' It was very beautiful, and of course I immediately agreed to sing it. I have a slight feeling that Eric wanted to sing the song himself, but I am very grateful that I got the chance to perform it."

Although it never really felt as though Davis's heart was in it, Arista U.S. stayed in the Iggy Pop business. Mr. Pop was a NYC resident at the time, living at the Iroquois Hotel, and making his third Arista album, *Party*, at the Record Plant with producer Thom Panunzio. Arista's head of artist development, Abbey Konowitch, recalls Iggy coming up to the office virtually every day. Tour publicist Jill Christiansen says, "I was just a fan, and they did the Tom Snyder show one night, and Dennis [Fine] said, 'You can't go,' because I guess we weren't supporting the album that much. It was like a 6 o'clock taping, and it was near the office, so I went after work. And I always had this red wool hat that I wore. On the last song they perform on the Snyder show, Iggy dances over and grabs my hat and puts it on, and I thought, 'My God, Dennis is going to see that.'" Christiansen also remembers a label meeting with Davis and the whole Arista executive staff. "Clive played new music, and he'd be so enthusiastic, and then he had to play something from *Party*, and Iggy had that song 'Pumping for Jill.' It had nothing to do with me. Everyone turns around and looks at me, and I'm like, 'Hey, it's not me.' If it were, I'd wear it like a badge of honor. I *wish* I could say Iggy Pop wrote a song about me."

Bud Scoppa's ventures with the Pop and the Bus Boys hadn't paid off (he also signed an L.A. band called Elton Duck that stayed in the vault for decades), but he did come across something with hit potential. "The thing that saved my gig was, Billy Meshel, who ran the publishing company, walked a single down to my office, and said, 'You should really send this to Clive. It's a group called Air Supply.' There was an overnight bag that we used, 'the pouch,' so I put in in there, and Clive was nuts about it. He thought it was a female singer, so I had to correct him on that score. They had hits, and

I had job security for a while. It was the furthest thing from my taste, and it was the only thing I could get arrested with."

Air Supply, a duo from Australia with schmaltz-level set to stun, helped Arista weather a transitional period, and in the fall of 1980, Clive Davis was putting an optimistic spin on the label's performance. Revenues, *Billboard* reported, jumped 69 percent over the previous summer's sales, and figures for July–August showed a 20 percent increase from the same period in 1977, "the company's previous all-time high." Davis said, "The gold and platinum figures we are reaching are encouraging signs that the industry is rebounding with health and vigor. Let's hope the recovery gets as much consumer newspaper space as did our stagnation."

One new signing he was particularly enthusiastic about was Aretha Franklin, who left Atlantic after a dozen years to join the Arista roster. She'd been languishing at Atlantic; her most recent album, *La Diva*, was her first since 1966 not to reach the Top 100, and she must have been looking around at upstarts like Donna Summer and Natalie Cole and fuming. She had *owned* the Grammy Award for Best Female R&B Vocal Performance. She won the trophy eight years running, but Cole had taken it twice since (1976 and 1977). Then Thelma Houston won it, then Summer. Enough was enough, and Franklin could see what Davis had done, turning around Dionne Warwick's career (her "Déjà Vu" was on track to win the R&B Grammy for 1979).

Was it a coup to whisk away the Queen of Soul from Atlantic, or was it folly? The album, just called *Aretha* (the name of her 1961 Columbia Records debut as well), with production duties split between Chuck Jackson and Arif Mardin, was slated for September 1980, just months after the premiere of the film *The Blues Brothers*, in which Aretha gave an electrifying performance of "Think." Davis sent out a hundred copies of the LP with a handwritten letter to "key tastemakers" to let them know this was hot stuff, and he invited U.S. wholesalers and foreign affiliates to an album preview. In the end, this label debut wasn't quite a jewel in Franklin's crown, but it was a start.

Aretha Franklin in *The Blues Brothers*, released the same year as her first Arista album.

LOVE (PLUS ONE)

IN 1976, ARISTA RELEASED *HISTORY OF BELL U.K. 1970–1975*, a compilation that included tracks by Hello, the Glitter Band, Gary Glitter, Showaddywaddy, Slik (with future Ultravox member Midge Ure), the Bay City Rollers, Barry Blue, and others. It's like a manifesto for a failed revolution, a map of an alternate pop universe. The whole glam thing, a specialty of Bell in England, pretty much skipped America, and with that, the idea of a second British Invasion petered out, which was sort of a shame, because the U.S. could have used a dash of loony stylistic excess in the early '70s. But very few glam records got on the radio, and America didn't have a chance to see what was going on. It's possible that if kids in the U.S. could have watched *Top of the Pops*, perhaps on Friday nights on ABC after *The Brady Bunch* and *The Partridge Family*, everything would have been different.

It was a changed world in the early '80s. MTV went on the air—not everywhere, not yet—in August 1981, with wall-to-wall music videos, and what everyone remembers about those embryonic years on the channel was how very British it was, out of necessity. MTV needed content, but American record labels weren't so invested in making music videos, so a lot of the programming was imported, and English artists started selling albums in the U.S. Around the same time, as Arista's L.A. marketing manager Dave Jurman points out, "Several things were in confluence. One was this new developing format of Modern Rock; you had stations that had been in existence for a while and switched to this new format: WLIR in New York, K-Rock in Los Angeles. That format just exploded and gave an anchor for artists who were not pop enough to get on Top 40 but were not really going to be put on AOR radio which was still playing Journey and Springsteen. And, fortunately for that format, MTV signs on August 1981 and had the videos for all those artists."

MTV wasn't on the cable system in New York City yet, so Arista executives, except for some who lived in the 'burbs, didn't have firsthand experience seeing the original "VJs." But they saw sales sheets. "What was bizarre," Jurman says, "is that MTV was in Dubuque, Iowa, places like that. And I remember us saying 'Why are we seeing Flock of Seagulls sales in Dubuque?' We're seeing sales in Appleton, Wisconsin." And then, according to Jurman, "There were these teen discos playing all this new wave stuff. You had Danceteria in New York, the Peppermint Lounge, the Melody in New Jersey. Those hybrid rock-slash-dance clubs. Iggy Pop's 'Bang Bang,' huge dance club hit." Matt Pinfield, who DJ'd at the Melody before and during his stint as the face of Modern Rock at MTV, says, "As much as I wasn't into the disco thing, you could actually build an incredible crowd playing alternative music and rock-oriented dance music."

All of this combined to make the start of the '80s a dizzying free-for-all, and all eyes were pointed towards the U.K. Arista made a distribution deal with Clive Calder's Jive Records, from where came the aforementioned A Flock of Seagulls. Arista's head of artist development, Abbey Konowitch, says, "They have a song called 'I Ran.' I brought it to the promotion team, we brought it to some radio programmers, and they said, 'We cannot play this song.' It was right after Iran held the U.S. soldiers [sic] hostage. … I said, okay, what if we call it 'I Ran' and put in parentheses 'So Far Away'? So when it was on the radio, it was called 'I Ran So Far Away.' What really made it special was, we hadn't made the video yet, and [lead singer] Mike Score got caught in the rain, and he just combed his hair in the shape of a seagull. And immediately, it became a buzz."

With the Seagulls coming from Jive, and Pete Shelley (of the Buzzcocks) and the Members added to the Arista roster as the result of a label deal with producer Martin Rushent—Shelley's "Homosapien" became one of those big rock-slash-dance club hits—the relationship between Arista in the U.S. and Arista U.K. was not always totally harmonious. Arista U.K., headed by Managing Director David Simone, with major creative contributions from A&R guy Simon Potts, was actively signing new acts, and Clive Davis was not always on board with releasing those acts in America. This had always been the case: Davis hadn't put out Max Merritt, or Fancy, and when Arista U.K. jumped on the neo-mod scooter in '77 and signed the Secret and the Pleasers, Arista U.S. shrugged. Most of the time, it was the right call. It wasn't likely that the Blues Band, fronted by Manfred Mann's Paul Jones, would have meant anything in America, and what's the point of a mod revival in a country where mod was never a thing? But when Simone and Potts signed the Stray Cats...

"Clive had to agree to put the records out," Simone says, "and I bring him the Stray Cats. He basically said, 'I don't get it.' I said 'Clive, you have to see them live.' They were playing this gig in New York, and I arranged for [top Cat] Brian Setzer to pick Clive up at the office and take him on his motorbike to Bond's, which was only like fifteen blocks. Show was sold out, I heard it was amazing. Clive passed."

Arista in America did pick up the Thompson Twins, and Haircut One Hundred, both signed out of the U.K. office. The Thompson Twins—none named Thompson, none related, not a duo—came through Hansa, a German label that Arista U.K. distributed. Simone recalls, "It was a very big band at the time. It was probably nine, ten, eleven people [more like six or seven, but it seemed like a lot more], and it was sort of African-tinged, and it was sort of cool. Simon signed them away from Hansa—I can't quite remember how it happened—and they started recording the album with a great producer named Alex Sadkin.

"What we did," he continues, "is through Robyn Kravitz [an Arista promotion person], we hired an independent—I even remember his name, Chris Nelson—to work the *Billboard* Dance chart, which in those days was really influential. And he took [the] Thompsons to number-one." "In the Name of Love" and "Lies," in fact, both hit the top of that chart, and "Love on Your Side" reached the Top 10. The group, now pared down to a manageable trio (Tom Bailey, Alannah Currie, and Joe Leeway), was on a path to U.S. star status (Top 40 hits, platinum album, Madison Square Garden, songs on soundtrack albums...). "It was really the Thompson Twins that got me a start as a product manager," Tom Ennis, an Arista artist development executive, says. "I became the guy who sort of went and dealt with it, and the exciting thing about the Thompson Twins was MTV was just huge, and they were a huge MTV band. I got to go to Atlanta because they're doing something for MTV, and I wound up hanging out with Martha Quinn. For us [it] was absolutely the case of it representing the apex of breaking a new British band." Ennis wound up accompanying the Twins to Philadelphia for their Live Aid appearance, where they did a version of the Beatles' "Revolution" with Madonna. "The great part," Ennis says, "was going to the party the night before. Everybody came. There were two towers in the hotel where everybody stayed, and you go up to the roof, and we had a grand ol' time."

Arista had equally high hopes, some would even say higher, for Haircut One Hundred, whose appeal is summed up by a speech by a character in John Carney's '80s-set musical play *Sing Street*: "Only a group of lads from a grubby suburb of South London would have the audacity to introduce the 1980s to a fuckin' xylophone. And not satisfied with this level of happiness, Haircut One Hundred throw this jazz-funk clarinet at ya as well! It's perpetual summer for these lads, even if they are all wrapped up in woolly jumpers and braces—they are the gods of joy."

They were a wellspring of delight, "these lads," fronted by the camera-ready Nick Heyward, who graced the covers of all the U.K. teen magazines. In England, *Pelican West* yielded three Top 10 hits—"Favourite Shirts (Boy Meets Girl)," "Love Plus One," and "Fantastic Day"—and it did look as though America might fall in line as well. You couldn't say it wasn't given a shot. "We were working six records," says Arista's rock promotion head Mike Bone, "and we had five of them on KMET. The sixth record was Haircut One Hundred. And so we took the program director and the music director from KMET out to lunch at The Palm, to celebrate this five-out-of-six thing.

"We had this private dining room in the back," he continues, "and we're having lobster and champagne. I said, 'What would it take to get this Haircut One Hundred record on KMET?' Sam Bellamy [the PD] said, 'What are you willing to do?' and I said, 'Tell me what I've got to do now, I'll do it.' 'Would you get a blue mohawk?' 'Yes.' She gets on the house phone there—this is pre-cellphone days—and calls her barber. 'My barber is going to be at the station when we get back.'

"The guy gives me a fucking mohawk and sprays it blue, and then sprays the side of my head silver. And I'm sitting there with this fucking blue and silver mohawk, I hear the record being played on the air. So I was like, 'Is it going to be in rotation?' She goes, 'Yes, four times a day for six weeks.'"

The first time Haircut played L.A., it was at the Roxy. Dave Jurman says, "There was a huge teen disco called the Odyssey. I said, 'Guys, would you mind coming and just doing a track performance after the show?' Like, 'Love Plus One,' or whatever. We get there, hundreds of people, jam-packed. The kids rush the stage. It was absolute bedlam. And I had to race them up to the office. I had the limo pull up behind and literally, it was right out of *A Hard Day's Night*, the kids chasing the limo with the boys and the band and stuff like that. That's how big it was." The next time Haircut hit town they were playing the 3,500-capacity Santa Monica Civic Auditorium. And even though *Pelican West* didn't take off in the States, they generated enough good will and momentum that they seemed poised to break.

They had so much going for them. The mainstream American press, prone to skepticism when it came to British sensations heralded by the U.K. music weeklies, was won over. Stephen Holden in *The New York Times* got a big kick out of a Haircut show at the Ritz, calling the group's music, "a cheerfully eclectic pop that blends rap, funk, Beatle-esque nostalgia, salsa and Talking Heads-style yelping into an all-inclusive international style not tied to a single sound." *The Boston Globe* chimed in, "They left a clattering, mouth-agape bunch of believers. ...The one-year band left no doubt about its future greatness." They made believers out of hard-to-please rock stations like WMMS in Cleveland, which aired a live broadcast; they were invited on *American Bandstand*.

THE EXCITEMENT OF HAIRCUT ONE HUNDRED!

Haircut One Hundred are the hottest band to hit Britain in eons. Their brisk, cheeky mixture of rock, pop and funk has sent two singles and their debut album zooming straight to number one on the charts. Their performances have sent fans into outbursts of spontaneous delight. And by special request of numerous venues across the country, Haircut One Hundred's live U.S. arrival is imminent.

America is already feeling the impact of Haircut One Hundred: "Love Plus One" is hit-bound from intense clubplay, and there are eleven other examples of their exuberant, original sound on their album debut, Pelican West.

Charts:
BB: 161*
Rockpool: 2*

In England, David Simone was eagerly awaiting a follow-up: "We had pre-orders from the biggest retailers on Haircut's second album, if we delivered it in time for Christmas, for 500,000 units. This would have done a million albums." In the U.K., that would have made it more than three-times-platinum. But there was internal strife within Haircut; Heyward split from the group and recorded a solo album, *North of a Miracle*. "I was heartbroken that Nick decided to leave," Jurman says, and he wasn't alone. Roy Lott, then Arista's head of business affairs, echoes Jurman and Simone: "If they had stayed together, they could have developed into something. They could've been Thompson Twins, easily, and with an even more attractive front guy. They could have been big."

Aside from the Thompsons, Haircut, and a few others, like Fashion and the Danse Society, most of Arista's British acts didn't come through the U.K. company, but through licensing deals, artists that Arista picked up for America. "One advantage we had," Lott says, "is because we were an indie, we could do a U.S.-only deal." Many U.S. labels were restricted in terms of outside acquisitions because their parent companies were interested only in grabbing worldwide rights. Davis didn't care about that, about Arista's owners making money from other territories. So representatives from English record companies could come to New York to peddle their wares, showing up in Davis's office with trendy aluminum briefcases filled with cassettes. "Simon Draper from Virgin would come in, and he would basically play two or three songs and say, if you wanted them, it'd cost something around a quarter of a million an album. This was before Virgin set up shop in the States."

Arista chose Heaven 17 from the Virgin grab-bag, and Jermaine Stewart on Virgin's 10 Records. Icicle Works, touted by Michael Barackman, came courtesy of Martin Mills and Beggars Banquet Records. There was the Martin Rushent deal. In addition to Flock, Jive provided a lively new-swing combo called Roman Holiday and Mama's Boys, a hard-rock band of brothers from Ireland, who were beaten out in the Slade-cover sweepstakes by America's Quiet Riot. Bram Tchaikovsky was signed to Radar in the U.K. In a way, it was like when Larry Uttal was constantly going back and forth to London to negotiate deals with Mickie Most, Larry Page, and Dick James, except in this case, Davis didn't have to get on a plane. There was, Lott says, something of a ticking-clock component to the meetings in his office. "The sellers would show up, at, like, high noon and say, okay, we have a 2:30 meeting [with another label]. Let us know by 2:30." Maybe in those couple of hours Davis would consult with members of his staff, maybe not.

Record companies in the U.S. suddenly had to generate their own videos. "That was a time," says Peter Baron of Arista's artist development department, who found himself navigating the new visual-musical universe, "when you really had to go with whatever singles the U.K. companies were doing, because if you didn't have a video, you didn't have a single, so they sort of forced our hands. In the early days, it was, 'Are we going to do a video for this song?' and then it became automatic. We were winging it, and nobody knew anything, and it's just a matter of having the eye for it and finding the right director for the right artist at the right budget. And I'm 24 doing this." And it wasn't just for MTV, Baron says. "There were local video shows in every major market, and people watched those videos. ABC affiliates in Chicago, New York, and L.A. had 11:30-at-night video shows, and that's where *Hot Tracks* started. *Friday Night Videos* had a much bigger reach, a much larger audience, than MTV ever had."

It was, most Arista alumni agree, an anything-goes period for the label, those first few years of the '80s. There was a spirit of *why the hell not*? A Bill Conti instrumental single of the theme from *Dynasty*? A loony patriotic—and eerily prescient—declaration "Let's Make America the Beautiful Again" by Michael Brogan? Manilow doing a neo-rockabilly tune ("Oh Julie") that was a U.K. hit for Shakin' Stevens? A hard-rock band from Switzerland (Krokus) with barely-English songs like "Long Stick Goes Boom"? A Meco "Big Band Medley"? A "comedy" album by Chevy Chase? All of those records came out in the early '80s on Arista Records, and no one has a sensible explanation for any of them (in fairness, Krokus, who came as part of the Ariola deal, did move a decent amount of product). It wasn't a great time for the music industry in general, and people looking to assign blame found scapegoats in the blank-cassette business (Arista announced it would not spend money on any retail ads that made reference to blank tape, like that

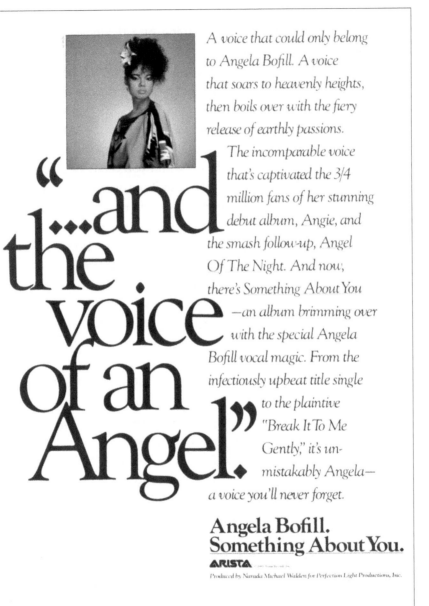

was going to keep kids from making and sharing mixtapes) and in video gaming (Clive Davis penned a *Billboard* editorial telling his fellow record execs not to panic).

Linking up Aretha with fan-producer Luther Vandross proved to be a shrewd move, even though the two did not always personally click. 1982's *Get It Right* was the QoS's first gold album in a half-dozen years. The Kinks came up with a handful of Ray Davies's best songs in quite a while on 1981's *Give the People What They Want* ("Better Things," in particular, is a lovely musical benediction). Davis matched the voice of Dionne Warwick with the songs and production of Barry Gibb and his brothers on *Heartbreaker*. But, overall, there was a sense of marking time, maybe missing a few opportunities. In the meantime, Davis did what might be considered a trial run for what was up ahead. He signed Angela Bofill directly, away from GRP, put her in the studio with producer Narada Michael Walden, and took the role of Executive Producer. The songs came from some of the top contemporary writers, and some familiar names: Cynthia Weil and Tom Snow, Allee Willis, Linda Creed and Thom Bell, Doug Frank and Doug James, as well as Walden and Bofill. *Something About You* is slick and youthful, rhythmic and melodic. It has MOR ballads like "Break It to Me Gently" and girl-groupish yearning ("Holding Out for Love"). It might simply be the case that Bofill was not ideal casting for this urban-pop musical formula, and the album was only a modest success. Davis had stepped into that territory before, tentatively with Linda Lewis, more tenaciously with Phyllis Hyman, but the right woman hadn't come along.

On Thursday July 23, 1981, GRP artist Dave Valentin was headlining at the Bottom Line, and a few Arista staffers were there to show support, among them Richard Smith, head of R&B Promotion; publicist Melani Rogers; and Gerry Griffith, a relatively new hire in the A&R department. The opening act was Cissy Houston. (Some narratives say the show was in 1980, but the Bottom Line website doesn't list an '80 Valentin-Houston gig.) As part of her set, Houston turned the mic over to her not-yet-eighteen-year-old daughter, Whitney. One of the songs the younger Houston sang was "Home" from the Broadway musical-turned-film *The Wiz*. Griffith has been quoted in interviews as saying that Smith turned to him and said he should sign that teenager. Griffith didn't think she was ready.

She'd been getting ready. Her mom, a member of the stellar gospel-R&B group the Sweet Inspirations, had started a solo career and was doing dates around the city. In the late '70s, she was on Larry Uttal's Private Stock label, and on her 1978 album *Think It Over*, produced by Michael Zager, Whitney Houston sang backing vocals on all but one song. She was featured on a '78 Zager track, "Life's a Party," had a spot in her mother's live shows at venues like Reno Sweeney (at one engagement, Cissy's opening act was Allan Rich, who went on to write "Run to You" for *The Bodyguard*) and did backing vocals on Cissy's Columbia album *Warning–Danger* (1979).

Gerry Griffith wasn't the only A&R person circling Whitney, who was also doing some modeling and lining up guest appearances on albums by Material (where she sang a song called "Memories," with Archie Shepp on saxophone) and Paul Jabara and Friends (doing the lead on "Eternal Love"). The industry was paying attention. As early as 1980, *Record World's Black Oriented Music* column touted Houston as "someone to keep an eye on." Nelson George, in his *Billboard* column *The Rhythm and the Blues*, in early 1983, wrote, "Whitney has shown a still-developing personal style, one that echoes her mother's soulful delivery, but with a cool pop quality of her own. Whitney has the pedigree and style to be a major vocalist."

When Griffith found out that Elektra Records, in particular, was zoning in on Houston, he decided to take a second look and attended another Cissy Houston show, at Seventh Avenue South, the Breckers' joint. This time, he was knocked for a loop by young Whitney, and alerted Clive Davis about the singer and the competitive interest. A showcase was arranged, and Griffith (according to a blog post where he recounts his Whitney saga) insisted that she close the set with "Home," her reliable showstopper.

Davis was impressed, which was hardly surprising, and went to see her soon after at Sweetwater's with friends. Few singers her age had so much poise and power; there was her mom's influence, of course, but she also had some of the steely confidence her cousin Dionne Warwick had when she, Burt Bacharach, and Hal David elevated the art of sophisticated pop-R&B, along with a gospel intensity that she'd honed singing with the New Hope Baptist Choir in Newark. And she was stunning. Davis would often reference Lena Horne as a Whitney precedent, and in another era, that would have probably been her path: nightclubs and movies, ritzy venues, elegant gowns. There was something classic about her. Who knows what type of artist she might have been had she signed with Elektra under Bruce Lundvall, a label president with vast knowl-edge and appreciation of jazz, what turns her music might have taken? For her ambi-tions, though, and those of her mom (there was an element of Mama Rose in *Gypsy* going on: "Sing out, Whitney!"), an alliance with Clive Davis was absolutely the way to go. And so, in the first months of 1983, Arista Records and representatives for Miss Whitney Houston (as her manager made sure she was credited in the announcement press release) hammered out a contract, which included, for the first and only time, a key man clause for Davis. If he were to leave Arista, Whitney could leave as well. The deal was closed in April.

Another contract was being negotiated at the same time. At the end of March 1983, Clive Davis dropped the news that RCA was acquiring 50 percent of Arista Records from its parent company, Bertelsmann, and that Arista would be switching from independent distribution to RCA's branch distribution. For the indie distributors, this news was devas-tating. A&M Records, once one of the most successful indie labels, had gone to the RCA branch system in '79, Chrysalis switched over to the CBS branch network in January '83, and Motown moved to MCA's branch system a few months after the Arista-RCA deal. As reported in *Billboard*, the news of the back-to-back defections of Chrysalis and Arista had the indies "accelerating steps to initiate legal action against the corporate parties." Davis, in a prepared statement, said, "As the industry changes, we have been looking into means by which we can continue to develop as a trend-setting viable company... The agreement with RCA will afford us the opportunity to maintain growth while remaining independent in terms of structure and style." Which was of small comfort to the distributors like Pick-wick, Schwartz Brothers, MS, and Piks. As recently as 1979, when the Ariola deal was made public, Davis had given assurances that Arista would stay an independent label. Now it was part of RCA, and although Davis did, as he indicated he would, operate creatively in the same way, with no change in the company culture, the switchover effectively ended the indie era that had begun with Bell Records and continued for nearly a decade after Davis formed Arista.

One footnote to that seismic event: For a while, around 1982, New York real estate developer Donald J. Trump, according to a 1984 *New York Times* piece, "was purchasing large amounts of RCA stock, with an eye toward securing a controlling interest, but he gave up on that when the price of the stock more than doubled. He sold the stock, profiting handsomely from the failed takeover." The mind reels at the thought of Trump being Clive Davis's boss, but fate had a different prank to play.

AND WHEN THE NIGHT FALLS...

FROM A PRACTICAL STANDPOINT, the Arista operation didn't change much. As Roy Lott points out, "Clive treated Arista as an indie. He was accountable to people, whether he wanted to acknowledge it or not, but I can tell you the times having to go to a BMG meeting and Clive wouldn't come." He had other things to do, like retool his entire executive structure and start to make a Whitney Houston album. When the Houston signing was trumpeted in spring 1983, the intention was to have an album out by the end of the year, but it became pretty obvious pretty quickly that that was never going to happen. First, Davis, Gerry Griffith, and the rest of the Arista A&R team needed to find songs and line up producers. In hindsight that seems easy enough, but in 1983 Whitney Houston wasn't *Whitney Houston*. The industry knew that Davis had anointed her—he had already introduced her to a national television audience on *The Merv Griffin Show*—but the songs that were coming in just didn't excite anyone, even after industry showcases on both coasts for the movers and shakers, the songwriters and music publishers. It was like the creative community didn't quite know what to make of her, wasn't certain where she fit in. That whole process would take some time, longer than anyone would have liked.

Arista, in the meantime, needed some internal shaking up. The financial picture leading up to the new RCA arrangement hadn't looked too rosy. Not that Arista was alone in its struggles. In 1982, the press was ablaze with stories about how gloomy the music industry was, and at a product presentation at the Roxy in Los Angeles, Davis called the reporting "outrageous" and "irresponsible." But numbers are numbers, and there wasn't any way to spin them. There were some records on the Arista schedule that did well—the Thompson Twins' "Hold Me Now," the Kinks' "Come Dancing"—but the label was flinging random ideas into the air. Melissa Manchester's "My Boyfriend's Back," the Angels' hit written by Gottehrer-Feldman-Goldstein, was a flashback to the girl group records of the early '60s; Davis matched up Manilow and Jim Steinman (the verbose *auteur* behind Meat Loaf's blockbuster *Bat Out of Hell*) on "Read 'Em and Weep," and it was sort of like in the '60s when Davis would have belters like Jim Nabors sing songs like "Both Sides Now," except now with a Bob Giraldi video featuring the singer wearing clown face. (There was also a big hit with a Steinman–Air Supply epic, where Russell Hitchcock sounds as though he's singing from inside a washing machine on spin cycle, and Steinman has just added too much fabric softener.) Arista signed Peter Allen, to a near-universal shrug.

In the summer of 1983, Davis made some changes, bringing in a new executive VP, Sal Licata, from Chrysalis. and a new head of Promotion, Don Ienner, who came from Millennium Records. "I get hired by Donnie Ienner," Sean Coakley recalls. "He's still at Millennium. He and I and Sal Licata started on the same day in August of '83. And I remember we had this meeting, and there was an imperative that we'd better find something out there that fits radio, that has a heartbeat. There wasn't a lot of stuff coming right away." Coakley, who was brought in from Atco Records to run the rock promo department under Ienner, also convinced Arista to hire his colleague at Atco, Paul Yeskel, to be his number-two national guy. They dove in, picked a Krokus track that did okay, worked the Kinks' thematic follow-up to "Come Dancing" ("Don't Forget to Dance") and records by Pete Shelley ("Telephone Operator"), Graham Parker ("Life Gets Better"), Manfred Mann's Earth Band ("Runner"), Icicle Works ("Birds Fly [Whisper to a Scream]"), and Heaven 17 ("Let Me Go").

Both Jim Cawley in Sales and Dave Jurman in Marketing mention Heaven 17 as one that got away. Cawley says, "If we had it to do over again, if somebody said, 'We're going to let you have a do-over for one record,' Dave Jurman and I would say the same record, Heaven 17's 'Let Me Go.' If that were a record where we had everything there, Donnie, everybody in Promotion and Sales doing a bolder campaign, gotten the group over, done a tour where they opened for Depeche Mode, whatever, it's possible, in my humble view, that album could have sold a million copies."

As he did when he launched Arista in 1974, Davis took out an ad in *Billboard*: "Arista's Brand New Marketing 'A Team' Is the Talk of the Industry!" the headline blared. In addition to the new recruits, the ad included headshots of Arista vets Lou Mann (Sales and Distribution), Dennis Fine (Media and Creative Services), Richard Smith (R&B Promotion), and Abbey Konowitch (Artist Development). (If anyone is keeping score, that's seven white males out of eight execs, zero women, so: progress?) It was this squad that would direct—with some changes and additions over the next six years—Arista's Promotion, Sales, Marketing, and Publicity efforts for the rest of the '80s. The turnaround wasn't immediate. The team was settling in, and Ienner's no-excuses, take-no-prisoners approach to promotion was paying off with singles by Billy Ocean and Whodini (both Jive artists) and Ray Parker Jr. ("Ghostbusters"). Cawley says, "Donnie understood sales better than any promotion person I ever knew. He has an incredible sense of how something could sell. He had an uncanny ability to sense what something could turn into."

One artist who Arista was pinning hopes on came in through Ienner's brother, Jimmy Ienner, who'd produced Arista hits for Eric Carmen and the Bay City Rollers. Janey Street, born in Queens, had been kicking around for a while, making records for Reprise and Capitol as half of the duo Janey and Dennis. She was shopping around a demo of songs for a solo record, and her attorney "sent everything out to like twenty million record labels, and they all were not interested, except for Jimmy Ienner," Street says. "He had a big production deal. He wanted me to do some rewriting, and he thought that some of the songs needed work, and everything he critiqued I fixed. Two minutes later, every record company wanted me, and he decided he wanted me to go with Clive." The album, *Heroes, Angels and Friends*, was like a New York City version of Rickie Lee Jones, with streetwise snap in songs like "Under the Clock" (a nostalgia piece with a doo wop pulse), "Say Hello to Ronnie," and "Jimmy (Lives in the House Down the Street)."

Peter Baron recalls, "Probably because it was produced by Jimmy, it had that stamp. I actually do remember that 'Under the Clock' video, I was the one who put that video together. I think VH1 was on the air then. ABC had a late-night show, they went up against *Friday Night Videos*, and it was a half-hour video show, and somehow, I convinced the producer to play that video, and that was like a big deal." There was something happening; for a minute, it looked as though "Say Hello to Ronnie" could make some noise in the fall of '84, but ultimately the momentum and the in-house enthusiasm waned, and Arista moved on. *Heroes, Angels and Friends* is like a punctuation mark between the old and the new Arista. Jimmy Ienner, with hits like Carmen's "All by Myself" and the Rollers' remake of Dusty Springfield's "I Only Want to Be With You," was a part of Arista's opening chapters, and Janey Street, an outer-borough singer-songwriter with a flair for narrative detail, was the type of artist that would have fit the Arista profile in the 1970s.

Closing another chapter, and coming around to his earliest influences, Barry Manilow ended his Arista tenure (for a short while) with late-1984's *2:00 AM Paradise Café*, a clue to where he might have gone, a road not taken. It's a relaxed, jazzy set, with guests including Mel Tormé, Sarah Vaughan, Gerry Mulligan, and Shelly Manne, and one track where Manilow added music to a previously unheard lyric by Johnny Mercer ("When October Goes"). He had been a linchpin of the Arista roster, the last remaining artist that Davis kept around from Bell. The year before, Melissa Manchester had made her final album for the label, *Emergency*, her first since 1975 to miss out on the *Billboard* Top 100 album chart. Arista's initial new signing, Gil Scott-Heron, was MIA after 1982's *Moving Target*; it would be more than a decade before he resurfaced with the album *Spirits*. Graham Parker put out his final Arista album, *The Real Macaw*, in 1983, and in 1984, the Kinks delivered their last for the label, *Word of Mouth*, featuring Dave Davies's best-known Arista track, "Living on a Thin Line," used in 2001 in the "University" episode of *The Sopranos*. With Patti Smith and the Grateful Dead still on hiatus from the recording studio, there wasn't much on Arista's release schedule, apart from the Alan Parsons Project and Ray Parker Jr. (for one more album), that resembled the label as it was in the second half of the '70s.

As 1985 approached, the whole world at 6 West 57th Street was about to flip, because Whitney Houston's debut album was, at last, finished.

"Her emotive style, which encompasses both a crystalline soprano and a lusty shout, is not well-suited to some of the pop material she attempts. And when she sings songs that do not really connect with her feelings, it shows." That quote is from a *New York Times* review of Cissy Houston by Robert Palmer, but it also predicted some of the response to her daughter. The accepted story of Whitney Houston is that when she signed with Arista and put her future in the creative hands of Clive Davis, she was steered toward the pop world. But you need to ignore a good deal of her musical background to come to that conclusion. When Griffith and Davis saw her, it wasn't as though she was Irma Thomas singing in an R&B club in the French Quarter of New Orleans. She was singing with her mom in Manhattan nightclubs, and Cissy was doing songs like "He Ain't Heavy, He's My Brother" and "You Light Up My Life." Whitney's own taste ran to "I Am Changing" from *Dreamgirls*, "Home" from *The Wiz*, and "The Greatest Love of All." Her ideas about show business came as much from Cissy as from Davis, and her mother was singing backup for Elvis Presley when his shows were, to a large extent, the majestic transformation of schmaltz.

Arista President Clive Davis introduces Whitney Houston in 1984 in New York City.

Photo by Michael Ochs Archives/Getty Images

One element of the Whitney game plan was about an idea of what was classy, how a young lady in the music industry ought to behave, and it's one thing to say that Davis and Arista had grandiose crossover dreams, which they certainly did, and another to pretend they were trying to turn Whitney into something she was not. If anything, Arista made an effort to muss her up a bit, make her less pristine, more youthful, sexier. The word was that Cissy objected to "Saving All My Love for You," Whitney's breakthrough ballad about stolen nights of passion with someone else's husband, because it might tarnish her image. ("Saving All My Love for You," originally done by Marilyn McCoo and Billy Davis, was written by Michael Masser and Gerry Goffin.) "The Greatest Love of All" wasn't Arista's idea. Houston walked in the door with it, since it was already a part of her step-out portion of her mother's gigs. In fact, the label stuck it on the B-side of "You Give Good Love," the record that established her at R&B radio. That track, written by LaLa, was produced by Kashif, as was the bright R&B-dance track "Thinking About You"; Kashif had come from B.T. Express and had previously worked with Evelyn "Champagne" King, Howard Johnson and Johnny Kemp—not exactly a pop résumé.

If Arista had wound up the *Whitney Houston* album with the sprightly, infectious single "How Will I Know"—a successor to such giddy early-'60s records as the Exciters' "Tell Him" and Betty Everett's "The Shoop Shoop Song," produced by Narada Michael Walden—and not gone back to rework "The Greatest Love of All," the album would have certainly sold fewer copies, but the cycle would have ended on a fresh and upbeat note. Roy Lott says, "'How Will I Know' was a big step. Gerry [Griffith] found that song when he and I were talking about the album and both said—at the same time—that she needed to record a song like 'Let's Hear It for the Boy' [the Deniece Williams hit from *Footloose*]. In other words, a potential pop hit that sounded young. Gerry flew to L.A. and came back with the demo. From the beginning, he and I always loved it. Whitney recorded all those vocals in one late afternoon."

It was the "How Will I Know" video, blasted around the clock on MTV, that brought out Whitney's playful side. "We were able to get Brian Grant to do it," Peter Baron says. "He had the magic touch with women." Among Grant's credits were videos for Kim Wilde, Olivia Newton-John, and Donna Summer, who, along with Tina Turner's *Private Dancer* videos, helped break the racial barrier for women on MTV with Grant's "She Works Hard for the Money." Baron says, "He wasn't one of those guys that wrote elaborate treatments. I remember him saying to me, 'Peter, I'm going to build a maze.' That's kind of how the whole thing was art-directed, her in a maze." Houston's "Saving All My Love for You" wasn't a natural fit for the channel, although they added it and gave it some screen time. "My mantra to Brian," Baron remembers, "really was 'MTV, this is going to be her breakthrough.' Let's make her young and hip and fashionable, and get around her lack of dancing, and I think we achieved that. We modernized her, basically, in that one video. If MTV would take any credit for Whitney, it'd be for 'How Will I Know.'"

Of course, Houston sang sweeping, melodic ballads; not letting her do so would be like forcing a thoroughbred to clip-clop jauntily around Central Park. But that's not where the heart of her debut was. It was on the Kashif-produced tracks, on "Someone for Me," where she's all alone and pining, waiting for rescue, and on the utterly disarming "How Will I Know." On those songs, she sounds as young as she was, just 21, her resolve balanced by vulnerability. You feel as though she's not trying to impress anyone, that she was as delighted as anyone by what her voice was capable of. (On the big ballads, Houston was more dutiful and pageant-like, although she never sang less than beautifully). What comes across on some of her records is caution and wariness, things that were evident when you met her, how she'd get a sense of the surroundings: *What does this person want from me?* Like she was trying to hold on to a piece of herself that was separate from the hubbub swirling around her. As Melani Rogers recalled to *Billboard*, "I was her first publicist. Before the release of her debut, she spent a lot of downtime in my office, between modeling and recording. She'd have a sandwich, sometimes take a nap, and we'd chat." Rogers adds, "She just wanted a place to get away from everything."

Whitney Houston is a brand of Extreme A&R, different from the way Aretha worked at Atlantic with Jerry Wexler, Dionne with Bacharach and David at Scepter. It wasn't like

Michael Jackson and Quincy Jones, or Donna Summer and Giorgio Moroder, where the artist and the producer pursue one vision. The album was important to the Arista Records story as a turning point, the moment when the trajectory of the label took off in a new direction. Marketing VP Abbey Konowitch says about Clive Davis, "Once he was focusing on grooming Whitney, that became his priority, and thank God it sold a shitload of records, but the tone of the company changed. And we became super-successful. But some of the spirit of adventure went out of it a little bit."

Whitney Houston was a sleek hit machine, assembled from disparate, non-cohesive parts, and once it went mega-platinum, it became a kind of music industry template (when Don Ienner went to Columbia, he and Tommy Mottola copied the Whitney playbook with Mariah Carey). There was so much more at stake now, there were so many compact discs (and videotapes) to sell, so many revenue heights to surpass, year after year. Arista, The New Record Company begun by Clive Davis as an independent label with so much promise from the legacy of Bell Records on Broadway, was more than a decade old, and was hanging plaque after platinum plaque on the walls of 6 West 57th Street, in the center of New York City.

POSTSCRIPT

I WALKED INTO THE DOORS OF ARISTA RECORDS in the sweltering summer of 1977, a freelance writer on music and movies, not long out of graduate school, and I really did think I was going to work at one of the coolest joints in town: the label that released Patti Smith's *Horses*, was bringing back the Kinks and the Grateful Dead, signing artists like Gil Scott-Heron, the Dwight Twilley Band, the Alpha Band, Linda Lewis, and General Johnson. Lou Reed was on Arista, and so was Rick Danko from The Band and Eric Carmen from Raspberries (I still had faith that "All by Myself" was an aberration). Arista owned the catalog of Savoy Records and released *Taxi Driver*, Monty Python, and *Saturday Night Live* albums. Where else would I want to be?

For years, I knocked out press releases, artist bios, and photo captions and then moved into creative services to do print and radio ads. (I won a Clio Award for a spot for a Monty Python album, but I was working in the studio with Eric Idle, so take that into account.)

Then, after a period of negotiation and exasperation, I was given the chance to try A&R. I found some songs for Arista artists, signed a few acts (the Church, the Jeff Healey Band), and A&R became my full-time career. That was at the end of this book's narrative, and the end of Arista as an independently-distributed record label. I left the label in 1993.

Arista is part of Sony now, under the stewardship of David Massey. It's gone through a bunch of incarnations since I last worked there nearly two decades ago. The thing about Arista, apart from it being the company that took a chance on me and gave me my career, and all that stuff, is that out of the scrappy little pop label that was Bell Records, Clive Davis built, brick-by-brick, a music empire. A little plaque at 6 West 57th Street would be nice.

ACKNOWLEDGMENTS

Many thanks to all the people who shared their Arista stories with me, the artists and executives who responded to my questions in person, on the phone or through e-mail. I asked them to dig for memories and stories from well over four decades ago, and considering what some of them were up to in those years, it's remarkable how much they were able to summon up. Gratitude to Eric Andersen, Michael Barackman, Peter Baron, Colin Blunstone, Mike Bone, Debbie Caponetta, Jim Cawley, Jill Christiansen, Sean Coakley, Michael Cuscuna, Ron Dante, Rick Dobbis, Tom Ennis, David Forman, Gregg Geller, Vernon Gibbs, Jeff Gold, Richard Gottehrer, Rose Gross-Marino, Richard X. Heyman, Dave Jurman, Lenny Kaye, Abbey Konowitch, Dennis Lambert, Mike Lembo, Arthur Levy, Roy Lott, Mike Mainieri, Willie Nile, Matt Pinfield, Bob Porter, Melani Rogers, Bud Scoppa, Marty Scott, Jules Shear, David Simone, Janey Street, Gregg Sutton, Jody Uttal, Tom Vickers, Alan Wolmark, Michael Zilkha and Jim Zumwalt. Not everyone made the final version of *Looking for the Magic*, but all contributed insight and context.

There were a few websites, American Radio History, 45cat, Rock's Backpages, that I can't imagine I'd have been able to piece the narrative together without. ARH, in particular, which has archived issues of *Billboard*, *Cash Box*, *Record World*, *Radio & Records*, *Music Business* and other music-related publications, was a source of vital information and in-the-moment perspective.

Some of what appears here was originally written, in different form, for the websites *Music Aficionado* and *Rock & Roll Globe*, so thanks to them for letting me riff on their spaces. I also had a blog, *Lost in a Fool's Paradise*, where some of my posts dealt with Arista-related matters, and I copped from that as well, as well as from liner notes I wrote for Arista reissues.

To my network of Arista colleagues, some of whom I count among my best friends, even if you are not quoted in here directly, please know that our shared experiences and our many, many conversations since have found their way into this volume. And from the moment I met him in August 1977, Clive Davis has been endlessly supportive and gener-ous. He gave this book his blessing and asked for nothing in the way of editorial input, for which I'm most appreciative.

Too many people from this Arista era are gone, and it'd have been great if their voices could have been among the witnesses. Among the missed: Dennis Fine, Michael Klenfner, Bob Feiden, Steve Backer, Marcy Drexler, Ben Edmonds, Milton Sincoff, Maude Gilman, and Lester Bangs, who came up to 6 West 57th Street a lot and was unsparing when he could tell he was being hyped. Having Lester living in New York at the time was a gift. He moved to Austin for a while, and he called me one afternoon at Arista, saying I had to come down there, that the social scene, the food, the music were all so much better. Before we hung up, he asked me to send him a copy of the *Taxi Driver* soundtrack album, and I took that to mean there were things about New York that he missed.

Special thanks to:
Scott B. Bomar at BMG Books, who thought this was a good idea and gave the green light
Ira Robbins at Trouser Press Books who took it over the finish line
Donna Cohen, who read, red-penciled and made it coherent

BIBLIOGRAPHY

BOOKS

Aletti, Vince. *The Disco Files* 1973-78

Arista Records Anniversary Celebration: 25 Years of Hits (Program Book Creative Direction: Ken Levy and Margery Greenspan; History & Artist Bio Writer: Arthur Levy)

Babitz, Eve. *I Used to Be Charming: The Rest of Eve Babitz*

Balls, Richard. *Be Stiff: The Stiff Records Story*

Blush, Steven. *New York Rock: From the Rise of the Velvet Underground to the Fall of CBGB*

Broven, John. *Record Makers and Breakers: Voices of the Independent Rock'n'Roll Pioneers*

Carlin, Richard. *Godfather of the Music Business: Morris Levy*

Christgau, Robert. *Christgau's Record Guide: The '80s*

Continuum Encyclopedia of Popular Music of the World, Volume 1, Media, Industry and Society

Dannen, Fredric. *Hit Men*

Davis, Clive and DeCurtis, Anthony. *The Soundtrack of My Life*

Fletcher, Tony. *All Hopped Up and Ready to Go: Music From the Streets of New York 1927-77*

George-Warren, Holly. *Man Called Destruction: The Life of Alex Chilton, From Box Tops to Big Star to Back Door Man*

Guralnick, Peter. *Sweet Soul Music: Rhythm and Blues and the Southern Dream of Freedom*

Hermes, Will. *Love Goes to Buildings on Fire: Five Years in New York That Changed Music Forever*

Hoskyns, Barney. *Glam! Bowie, Bolan and the Glitter Rock Revolution*

Jones, Roben. *Memphis Boys: The Story of American Studios*

Katz, Mike and Kott, Crispin. *Rock and Roll Explorers Guide to New York City*

Porter, Bob. *Soul Jazz: Jazz in the Black Community*

Quatro, Suzi. *Unzipped*

Ritz, David. *Respect: The Life of Aretha Franklin*

Rogan, Johnny. *Ray Davies: A Complicated Life*

Sachs, Lloyd. *T Bone Burnett: A Life in Pursuit*

Scott-Heron, Gil. *The Last Holiday: A Memoir*

Shapiro, Peter. *Turn the Beat Around: The Secret History of Disco*

Shaw, Philip. *Patti Smith's Horses*

Sidran, Ben. *Ben Sidran: A Life in the Music*

Sounes, Howard. *The Life of Lou Reed*

Spence, Simon. *When the Screaming Stops: The Dark History of the Bay City Rollers*

Swenson, John (editor). *The Rolling Stone Jazz Record Guide*

Trynka, Paul. *Iggy Pop: Open Up and Bleed*

Wainwright III, Loudon. *Liner Notes*

Whitburn, Joel. *Top Pop Singles 1955-1996*

LINER NOTES (in addition to original liner notes on arista album releases)

Dahl, Bill. *Get Low Down! The Soul of New Orleans '65-'67* (Sundazed)

Dahl, Bill. *Looking for My Baby! Soul Treasures From the Vaults of Amy-Mala-Bell* (Sundazed)

Dahl, Bill. *Aaron Neville – For the Good Times, the Allen Toussaint Sessions* (Fuel)

Dahl, Bill. *The O'Jays: I'll Be Sweeter Tomorrow, the Bell Sessions 1967-1969* (Sundazed)

Fisher, Bob. *James & Bobby Purify: The Complete Bell Recordings 1966-1969* (Soul Music)

Gibbon, Peter. *Deep in the Philly Groove* (Kent)

Heatley, Michael. *Music for the Millions – Gems From Bell Records USA* (One Day)

Henderson, Alex. *Martha Reeves* (Soul Funk Classics)

Kirkman, Jon. *Linda Lewis – Hampstead Days* (Troubadour)

Prangell, Laurence. *Shirley Brown* (Soul Brother)

Rounce, Tony. *General Johnson – The Best of the Arista Years* (Edsel)

Scorsese, Martin. *Taxi Driver Original Soundtrack Recording* (Arista)

Staunton, Terry. *The Alpha Band – the Arista Album*s (Acadia)

Waring, Charles. *Ben Sidran* (BGO)

Wikane, Christian John. *GQ Standing Ovation: The Story of GQ and the Rhythm Makers (1974-1982)* (Big Break)

WEBSITES

American Radio History
www.americanradiohistory.com

Both Sides Now
www.bsnpubs.com

The Bottom Line
www.bottomlinecabaret.com

45cat
www.45cat.com

Rock's Backpages
www.rocksbackpages.com

Secondhand Songs
www.secondhandsongs.com

Wikipedia
www.wikipedia.org

Original ads and records from the author's collection

ABOUT THE AUTHOR

Mitchell Cohen has written on music and movies for *Creem*, *High Fidelity*, *Phonograph Record*, *Film Comment*, and *Country Music*. He is the co-author of Matt Pinfield's memoir, *All These Things That I've Done*, and, with Sal Maida, *The White Label Promo Preservation Society*. He has done A&R for Arista, Columbia, and Verve Records, written liner notes for reissues by the Ramones, Jerry Lee Lewis, Whitney Houston, Maxwell, and others, and was nominated for a Grammy Award as one of the producers of *Sony Music 100 Years: Soundtrack for a Century*.

CPSIA information can be obtained
at www.ICGtesting.com
Printed in the USA
LVHW060452280522
719946LV00015B/424

9 798985 658903